WOLVES AT NIGHT

SARA MCDERMOTT JAIN

Identifiers:
LCCN: 2021915094
ISBN: 978-0-578-95689-3 (paperback)
ISBN: 978-0-578-95690-9 (hardback)
ISBN: 978-0-578-95691-6 (ebook)

For my son

1

THE JOURNEY

She had never been there in the dark months, with snow covering the ground. She'd only been there in the sun, when it stayed out almost eighteen hours a day.

There was nothing in her memories of off-roading with Ben that brought any familiarity to the dark, dense woods, now seen through a lacy veil of swirling snowflakes. In the dark, this route was unrecognizable.

"Bet you don't get dark like this down in the lower forty-eight," Chaz said, switching gears and hitting the truck's high beams. For the first leg of the trip, he'd left the lights off entirely so they could sneak their way out of town undetected . . . not that Eleni thought too many people were out to call in a hot tip on Ben Wilton anymore. Her jaw was still sore from clenching her teeth as Chaz went over the old Gold Rush Bridge, which didn't have any guardrails and was barely wide enough for a regular car. It wasn't built for cars at all, actually; it was there for anyone who wanted to cross the river from the small town—less than a square mile of houses and bars—and go out on the trails. She'd let out an involuntary shriek when the wooden planks groaned and cracked under the truck's weight.

Chaz had simply laughed at her. His truck had rolled onto the gravel on the opposite bank, rattling and bouncing over tree roots and rocks that had tumbled down from the mountains. He'd driven toward what seemed an impenetrable wall of Sitka spruce, only to wind his way through the trees and onto an obscure dirt road.

Now, Eleni gave a half-hearted smile and rubbed her sore neck. She'd barely slept since getting the message about Ben a day and a half earlier. It came as priority mail, Chaz likely not wanting to risk any police monitoring of her email or phone. The envelope was oversized and padded, containing only a hand-scrawled note written over the course of three green index cards that were paper-clipped together.

Gonna be at the cabin Tuesday night and wants to see you. And the kid. If you're gonna come, just email me time on Tuesday night for ferry. No details. —C

It was obvious Chaz had purposely tried to make his lettering look boxy so that, if pressed, he could deny it was his handwriting. He'd also put a fake return address on the puffy envelope.

This was it.

After some hasty packing, she'd driven several hours to a Seattle airport hotel to catch some broken sleep before an early flight. She'd gotten to Juneau around lunchtime, only to take the long ferry ride up the fjord to get to the deserted Alaskan tourist town where, several summers prior, she'd worked as a tour guide on an old railway system. Throughout all of it, she'd had to lug bags and, of course, Jacob—the two-year-old who now slept on her lap. She'd somehow assumed Ben would have told Chaz to have a car seat, then wasn't sure why she'd expected that of him.

"So, you excited to see our boy?" Chaz continued. He glanced back at her again, and she wished he would just keep his eyes on the dirt that passed for a road.

Eleni cleared her throat and nodded.

"What, speechless with anticipation?" Chaz chuckled as the truck rocked again.

"No, of course, I'm excited," she squeaked. Her eyes darted to the left as the truck swerved close to the edge of a steep drop off that bordered the woods. The frigid fjord was below. "Just . . . it's been a long time."

"Not holdin' nothin' against him, are you?" Chaz asked before snorting, rolling down his window, and hocking a ball of snot out into the frosty night air. Eleni suppressed a gag.

"No. It wasn't his fault."

"That's right. Ol' boy been set up—we all know that. He had to keep his head down, or they woulda sent him up for ten years or more."

Eleni looked down at Jacob's sweet face in her lap. His cheeks, still boasting the adorable fleshiness of babyhood, jiggled slightly with the motions of the truck. He breathed easily, steadily, and for that, she felt grateful. She pulled off one mitten and ran the back of her hand gently over one of his cheeks; the feel of the soft newness of his skin was instantly calming.

"He's never met Jacob," Eleni said. She wasn't sure if she actually wanted to talk about it with Chaz as much as she wanted to state it out loud and let it be known that the man she'd spent that Alaskan summer with three and a half years ago had never seen this boy. He wasn't there when she'd been screaming in labor or when Jacob came home as a small, swaddled bundle—such a home as it was. She'd set up a second-hand crib in the corner of a tiny studio apartment in a city near her hometown, down in the lower forty-eight. It was a far cry from the nursery she'd always envisioned setting up for her firstborn, but, like an animal, she'd gone to where she felt safest to give birth.

Ben wasn't there during the nights filled with Jacob's wails and constant feedings, the daycare drop-offs and pick-ups, or the early morning hours when, desperate for rest, she gave up and let Jacob sleep beside her in her bed, despite all doctors' advice against it. Ben missed solid foods and first words and crawling. Yet she always had this sense of pride, of showing the imaginary Ben how well she was doing—as if he were sitting in a corner of the studio, watching and smiling. His dreamed-up approval gave her confirmation that she was an amazing woman. Validation came at her through his imagined eyes.

"Had to keep his head down," Chaz repeated as if shaming her for pointing out that Ben had never met his son. The son who would turn three in June, just three months from now. Then his tack abruptly switched, and he looked back at her again. She really, really just wanted his eyes to stay on the non-existent road.

"So, guess it's been a while for you, huh?" he said, grinning. His teeth weren't practical-joke terrible, but there was definitely something off-putting about them; the tar of a million smoked cigarettes lined their crevasses.

The truck jolted and bounced violently. Jacob's eyes opened as his head knocked against his mother's lap, then closed again as Eleni gripped him tighter.

"Well, between work and the baby. . ." she trailed off, not wanting to have this conversation.

"Tonight's gonna be a good homecoming for ol' Ben," Chaz drawled, slowing the truck to get through a tight bend around a tree.

"If he gets here," Eleni said faintly. She'd spent a day and a half in transit, but Ben's arrival was uncertain as always. Maybe he'd deem the risk unnecessary.

"Hope you waxed," Chaz said, thoroughly entertaining himself. Eleni kept her eyes trained on the passing forest. "You know, I can always wait with you." He briefly turned to smile at her again, the black outlines around his teeth visible in the dashboard's glow. His head was tilted suggestively downward.

"No, we'll be ok," she said.

"Can be scary waiting all alone out here in the dark."

"We'll be in the cabin."

"Would get the better of some chicks," he said, eyes flashing to her in the rearview.

"I've been there before."

Just then, to their right, something dark and large bounded past the window, nearly slamming into them.

"Shit," Chaz spat, swerving and nicking the side mirror on a tree. "They're out in force."

"What are?" Eleni squinted out into the woods. Nearly half a dozen other large, hulking creatures darted among the trees within thirty yards of the truck, all galloping toward some shared destination.

"The wolves," Chaz said, taking sheer delight in delivering the information. He gave her a slow, purposeful, tar-laced grin. "The wolves are out."

Eleni searched the dark furtively, but the wolves raced out of sight.

"Ben ever tell you that's my job? Pick off the wolves that come up on those guys working over at the quarry. Always need a watch around here."

Eleni shook her head wordlessly.

"Why I always carry this," Chaz reached for the passenger seat floor. *Eyes on the road, eyes on the road,* Eleni's thoughts hissed, although it really couldn't even be considered a road anymore; tree branches grazed both sides of the truck as it continued to barrel forward in the snow, windshield wipers groaning as they pushed the flakes away, leaving behind frosty streaks.

When Chaz straightened up, he held a long, gleaming rifle. Cold pulses ran down Eleni's spine.

"That's been up there the whole time?" she asked as Chaz snickered. "Is it loaded?"

"Wouldn't be much use if it wasn't," Chaz said, putting it down. Eleni realized she'd unconsciously covered one side of Jacob's head and face—the side closest to the gun—with her hand. The knuckles of her other hand, gripping Jacob's puffy winter coat, were clenched inside her mitten.

She took a deep breath to calm down. The cabin had bars on the windows, after all, specifically because of the animals out here—Ben's idea. She'd be fine. Chaz probably knew how to handle the gun if that was his job.

The truck jounced again, and she worried if they bounced wrong, the gun could go off.

"I never saw wolves here before," she ventured, hoping they were almost there.

"You heard what happened on the train, though?"

She'd heard. It was one of those famous stories in town and one she'd shared with fascinated folks from the lower forty-eight many times as a tour guide. An avalanche had stopped the train in its tracks. The snow was only as deep as the windows, and everyone was ok at first, but then the wolves had come. They paced, waiting for their opportunity, breath fogging the windowpanes. They were eye to eye with the passengers inside, only glass between them. After a few hours, they tested the glass. The people inside watched, helpless, wondering how long it would take the animals to get in. Eventually, one wolf had charged and cracked the window like thin ice. It charged again and created a small hole, ignoring the bleeding gashes on its snout as it pushed through the splintered outline of the opening.

Wolves were like that. They could always see their "in."

Luckily for the passengers, a helicopter came and airlifted them, one by one, out of the rooftop emergency hatch before the wolves broke through. Five more minutes, though, and the story would have ended differently.

"I heard."

"Well, they're boldest right now, with the snow and all. Less food around. New pups being born now we're into March. But don't worry. Ben really fortified the cabin."

She knew bars on windows weren't typical, but Ben hadn't taken any chances. It was because of how much he loved her, how he'd never forgive himself if anything happened to her. That's why she'd always had to stay inside unless he was with her. She thought about summer, about sitting on the bed in the cabin, watching him chop wood from between the white-painted bars. She remembered when he'd come back in, sweaty and smelling like the woods, and lay on top of her, pressing her into the bedsprings. She could still feel the creaky loops of the springs spaced up and down her back.

The truck pulled beyond the fingers of the branches draped over the windshield, and the cabin was there, barely discernible in the dark. As they crept closer, the headlights flushed its façade, and it fell drastically short of what she remembered from that love-drenched, sun-soaked summer. In her memory, it was bright, cloaked in green. Now the front porch sagged, and the windows stared back dull and lifeless—nothing but a gray-black beyond the glass. The bars, spaced three inches apart on each window, had patches of rust poking like leprous sores through their rotted white paint, and the wood of the door looked chipped and faded. Several shingles hanging above the porch had slipped down to the boards, while others dangled precariously on the edge, threatening to fall at any moment.

"Generator working?" she asked, suddenly realizing there might be no heat or light. If Ben didn't come tonight, she and Jacob would be shivering, alone, and in the dark.

"Sure hope so—for your sake." Chaz laughed, putting the truck in park and taking up his rifle again. Then he saw her expression. "I checked it out this morning. Took a few minutes to get going, but it was good. Put the pilot light on, too, for the water heater."

"What if . . . what if Ben doesn't come?" she asked.

"I'll come back again to check you tomorrow. Unless . . ." He lifted his eyebrows at her. "Unless you want me to stay?"

She shook her head, fast. Then, feeling rude at how quickly she'd responded, she sputtered, "No, no. You should get back to town. In case anyone saw your truck come up here."

He nodded. "Yeah, yeah. I know you just want to see your man."

Her man.

"It's bizarre to think of him as 'your man,'" Tiff, her girl-friend back home, told her. They worked together, answering phones in a doctor's office—a pale manifestation of Eleni's desire to have a career helping other people. Like so many other things in her life, her vocation hadn't been fully formed. "You haven't seen him in over three years. You've had a kid since then."

It *was* bizarre. Yet she did still think of him as "her man." Was that because she hadn't been with anyone else since or because they'd never officially ended things?

Or was it because she really did, in fact, love him? Is this what love was? Because here she was, in the remote Alaskan wilderness at his off-the-grid cabin, just on the off-chance she might get to see him, might get to show him his son for the first time, might get to replace that imaginary Ben with a flesh and blood one and hear him say "you're an amazing woman" for real.

Hear it from the person who really mattered.

She'd told herself many times that yes, of course, this is what love was. This was the father of her child, so it had to be love. And everything that had happened . . . well, it was just their crazy story, their trial they had to get through that would bond them together forever. Like the storybook marriages she read about where people toasted their fiftieth wedding anniversaries with champagne. That was what she wanted. The forever love—to be a goddess to someone.

Chaz held down the clunky button for the truck's squeal-ing moon-roof, angling himself to stick his upper-half out.

"What're you doing?" Eleni asked as he positioned himself to stand up. He looked at her, incredulous, gripping the rifle.

"Well, I gotta keep watch," he told her. *Silly girl.* "It's gonna take you time to get all your stuff in. Get your kid in."

She looked around, out of each window in turn.

Chaz lowered his voice for emphasis. "Wouldn't want the wolves to get you."

2

UNLOADING

She would have hesitated longer if he wasn't watching her. That first tentative step, putting her booted foot down into the snow, was nerve-wracking. She kept imagining a wolf lying in wait right under the truck, ready to lunge and snap her foot off at the ankle the moment she hit the ground. That was impossible, of course; they'd only just pulled up over the small, cleared patch in front of the cabin. But still, putting that foot out made the nerves in her ankle jump, prepared for teeth.

Eleni left Jacob sprawled on the back seat of the car, still asleep, his cheeks flushed pink from the dry heat pumping through the vents. She'd eased herself out from under him, postponing another second, two, three, as she debated whether to take him in first or last. Last—she didn't want to have to fumble with the lock with Jacob in her arms, knowing the wolves watched from beyond the trees.

"Here," Chaz had said as she prepared to step out, dropping a set of keys into her mittened palm. The clunky keychain was one of those colorful, plastic-laced strips kids would make at camp, the end of it just beginning to come undone. She left the keys with Chaz three years ago, when she'd left town, so he could check on the cabin from time to time, and couldn't help notice he'd added a second keychain to the loop. It was sterling silver, molded into the shape of the upper half of a winking, busty woman, her nipples covered with two star-shaped pasties. Eleni closed her hand around it and pushed open the door.

One boot down, crunching into the snow, then the next, and she felt the sting of the glacial air against her cheeks. She shut the heavy door behind her but kept her back pressed against the truck's solid metal body. Chaz, from his crow's-nest position, laughed at her.

"Just get the stuff. I got you."

She never quite got the knack for packing, especially now with a small child. Jacob needed so many things, and she found it almost impossible to strip down to bare essentials. There was Jacob's food, Jacob's medicine, Jacob's toys, her stuff, and the bags of groceries Chaz took her to get before heading to the cabin.

Eleni had kept her head down in the store, not wanting to be recognized. Regrettably, the food had already been picked over. The store only got stock delivered once a week by barge, and if you didn't go on the first day, most things would be gone. She remembered from her summer all those years ago that if she waited until mid-week to shop, she'd have to resign herself to meals cooked from dried beans and powdered milk.

She didn't own a fancy luggage set, so everything was spread out: toys and food wrapped in plastic bags, medicine in a faded, over-the-shoulder bag originally intended for baby bottles, a backpack, a rolling suitcase, and a duffle bag. The back of Chaz's truck was open to the night sky, so everything was now covered with a dusting of snow.

"C'mon, now," Chaz urged, eying the trees, his rifle up and at the ready. Eleni thought of how easy it would be for him to turn it on her if he wanted to.

Ben owned a gun. He'd shown it to her that summer, aiming it directly at her face, then laughing at her expression. "It's not loaded, sweets."

She still remembered looking down the black hole of the barrel, seeing it was trained exactly, squarely, on her. Those cold pulses were back on her spine.

"Be quick," Chaz said, patience wearing thin.

She slung the backpack over one shoulder and the duffel bag over the other.

"Women can't pack for shit, that's for sure," Chaz murmured. Eleni couldn't tell if he was joking with her or genuinely irritated.

She grabbed a plastic bag filled with toy trucks and dinosaurs in one mittened hand, the other hand holding the keys. Turning, she carefully picked her way over rocks concealed by snow and headed for the door.

The steps up to the porch had warped since the last time she was here. They sagged down in the middle, and fringy lichen had sprouted along their edges. She wondered if anyone, including Chaz, had even been in here in the years since she'd packed her bag in late September and been driven into town by the police. From the looks of it, the building had stood neglected until Chaz checked the generator that morning. As if reading her mind, Chaz shouted out, "You might want to dust."

She made it to the door without glancing around the perimeter, despite the dozens of phantom wolf eyes that she imagined were following her. *Just stay focused, just get in.* She held the keys up to the rusty lock and shoved one in, metal grinding against metal. It wouldn't turn.

"Shoot," she said, trying to wiggle it. Nothing.

She put the plastic bag on the porch, followed by the duffel bag. Two-handed now, she worked it, wiggled it, and pushed against the door.

Still nothing.

"It won't open!"

"Well, I can't leave my post."

Deep breath. She pulled the key out and shook her hands a bit. Back in the lock. More wiggling. This time, it turned about a quarter inch—maybe it was just frozen. She exhaled on it, hoping her warm breath might thaw it out.

"Any progress?" Chaz called out.

"A little," she said, trying again. The lock squeaked as it finally turned. She threw the whole of her weight against the door, and scraping against the door frame, it pushed open.

She stumbled in as stale, cold air enveloped her. She wasn't sure how, but it felt a few degrees colder inside than outside. There was total darkness within; only the light of Chaz's headlights illuminated a sliver of the stone fireplace that reached up to the rafters. Her mitten fumbled at the light switch, then an overhead bulb buzzed on, giving one or two small pops before providing steady light.

There was dust everywhere, along with the oppressive feeling of a space untouched by human breathing . . . but overall, it was exactly as she remembered it, every detail, every accent.

To her right, only feet from the door, was a queen-sized mattress on a collapsible bed frame, a dusty multi-colored quilt thrown over it. The bed was pressed long-ways against the wall, below a window overlooking the porch.

Across from the bed was the fireplace, a two-story-tall stone tower situated between the door to the bathroom and the ladder to the loft. The ladder had flat, wide rungs and slanted toward the upper level like it wanted to be a staircase. The loft contained old boxes of papers, random storage, and another, smaller mattress. She'd needed to stoop when she was up there, which hadn't been often. The wooden ladder, fastened to the wall with two bolts up near the top, looked unsteady and partially rotted. It stood between the fireplace and the entryway to the small, makeshift kitchen.

To the left of the front door was a small area with a two-seater dining table and a side table against the back wall with a red tablecloth draped over it, hanging to the floor. The cabin had a symmetrical appearance from the outside, and a window was centered in the wall near the dining table, just as a window was centered over the bed on the other side.

Chaz honked his horn in one sharp blast, and Eleni winced, hurrying to drop the bags on the bed. The springs creaked under the weight as she rushed back out.

"In and out, let's go!" Chaz yelled. Eleni strained to see whether or not the horn had woken Jacob up. It didn't seem like it, but that might not be a good thing; when he slept through anything loud, it was usually because he was coming down with something. He'd just had a long journey, though, so he was hopefully only exhausted.

She clopped down the porch steps, feeling them bounce slightly beneath her weight, then froze when her boots hit the ground. Past the truck, in between the trees that encircled the small property, she caught a flash of two feral eyes watching her. Other sets of eyes flashed, one after the other, as the creatures moved silently between the tree trunks.

"I see 'em—don't worry," Chaz said, his gaze sweeping the woods. "They're there, all right, but I got 'em. Keep going."

When Eleni's feet moved again, it was as if they moved without her brain giving the signal, purely based on Chaz's orders. She felt disconnected, as if she were simply watching this woman from a distance, who, in going closer to the car, was actually going closer to the wolves.

When she reached the truck bed, she had to turn her back to the eyes she had just seen. Despite the frigid temperature, a trickle of sweat fingered its way down her spine. Her arms, as she loaded them with grocery bags, were awash in pinpricks.

"Go, go," Chaz ushered her on as if that was part of what helped him keep track of the whole situation. Eleni glanced in the back of the truck to see Jacob—oblivious and sprawled out with mittened fists balled up by his face—then trotted back toward the cabin.

"Next time, close the door behind you," Chaz called after her. "One of those gets in there, we won't be able to get it out without meeting face-to-face."

Eleni moved faster, then willed herself to move more calmly . . . swift but calm. Running in front of a predator tended to set off their chase reflex.

She was back up the stairs, swinging the door shut behind her, barreling back to the tiny kitchen. Along its back wall was a white, half-sized refrigerator, a relic from decades past, and a battered-looking gas oven and stove. A deep, stainless-steel sink had an old-timey water pump arched over it. She remembered how Ben purchased specifically designed pipe insulation to keep the water pipes from freezing.

Eleni awkwardly shoved the grocery bags onto the tall, wooden block of a table in the center of the floor—no stools or seats around it—and turned back right as she heard Chaz give a sharp "Gah!"

Her stomach dropped. She ran to peer out the front window, half-expecting to see a wolf clambering its way through the truck's moon roof, Chaz lying over the windshield with his throat ripped out.

He still stood at his post.

She came back out, woozy, heart pounding, and lightly shut the door behind her.

"See the snow over there?" He jerked an elbow toward a patch of disturbed snow near the trees without lowering the gun. "One tried to step out. Yelled at him, and he got back."

Eleni swallowed, her dry throat aching. If it had stepped out only moments ago, there was nothing to say it wouldn't step out again. Now that it had evaluated the situation, it might become more aggressive the next time.

They always saw their "in."

"Waitin' there like a sittin' duck don't help," Chaz called.

She started down the steps again.

This time, she moved slowly, scanning the almost 360 degrees of forest. She reached out for the truck bed like it was a life preserver, hooking her fingers over it, drawing herself close. She couldn't feel her fingers; they bumped against each other like dead flesh inside her mittens. It took three tries to grasp the strap of the medicine bag. Grabbing the handle on her rolling suitcase, she jerked it toward her, dragging it across the truck bed in bumps. She hoisted it out and around the ledge, feeling like she might collapse, then turned and headed back for the door. The dusting of snow that had gathered on the suitcase drifted to the ground.

"All right, one more to go," Chaz said, continuing his running commentary. Then Eleni heard it—a faint snarl from the trees.

Back up the stairs. Shoulder against the door, pushing it open. Shoulder against the door, pushing it shut. Suitcase at the foot of the bed, medicine bag on the dining table. Small clumps of snow from the duffel bag and backpack, which she'd left on the bed, had eased down toward the quilt, dampening it. She cleared the bed off, putting them on the floor with the suitcase.

Space heaters. The space heaters needed to be turned on. There was one up by the head of the bed, an old one, not one of the safer, newer models. She worked the dial, and it began to hum, the electric coils inside slowly turning red. She'd have to make sure Jacob didn't touch it. There was another one in the dining area, a third back in the kitchen. Each one stood like a small metal guard in its appointed corner.

Back to the front door. She rested her hand on the knob and took a deep inhale, pushing the air back out with force. Every inch of her ached, particularly her mid-back, the muscles behind her lungs. The deep breaths acted like an internal massage on her sore, fraught insides.

This was it. Jacob was all that was left.

3
THE FIRST DEATH

She closed the door behind her but didn't pull it hard. She didn't want to struggle with it when she made it back, Jacob's weight in her arms, clutched across her and stiff inside all of his winter clothing. The door was closed enough to keep a wolf from seeing the opportunity.

She did another sweep of the yard. There may have been a flash of eyes off to her left, but then again, her own eyes might have been playing tricks on her. The moonlight may have just caught on fallen snow, or a clump may have fallen from a tree branch, flashing in the refracted light from the truck.

Back down the steps, one foot at a time, purposefully, decidedly, one in front of the other. Chaz aimed his eye over the barrel of the gun.

"That it, then?" he asked as she came up beside the truck. She rested a hand on the door handle, not yet opening it.

She looked up at him with wide eyes.

"What will Ben do when he gets here? I don't have a gun. How's he gonna get in?"

Chaz snickered, taking his eyes off the trees briefly to enjoy the fear in her face.

"You think Ben doesn't know how to handle himself out here?"

There had certainly been plenty to indicate Ben was every inch the rugged outdoorsman, able to survive against all odds. He'd told her how bears killed down by the river tasted more like salmon, and those killed up in the mountains tasted more like honey. She'd never actually seen him defend himself, but she'd seen him attack.

Deep breath. Achy back. One last check behind her, and she opened the truck door, fully exposing Jacob to whatever might be outside with her.

She pulled him a bit closer to her by his feet, then took him up in her arms.

"Hey baby, hey baby," she cooed as his eyes fluttered half-open. He focused on her for only an instant before closing his eyes again, this time leaning his head fully against her shoulder. She hitched him up securely, then slammed the door shut . . . and turned.

"Don't worry," came Chaz's voice. "I got him."

Twenty feet from her and Jacob, eyes fixed on them from just beyond the first line of trees, was a massive gray wolf. Any other wolves were lost in the shadows, but he was right on the fringe of cover, confident and intrigued.

"Oh, God," Eleni breathed, back against the car. Jacob stirred as he adjusted himself against her shoulder, then snored. She saw the animal's breath coming in smoke signals as it breathed in and out. Its fur shifted in the wind, peppered with snowflakes.

"Just keep on," Chaz instructed. "I got him."

She slinked along the truck toward the cabin as if the simple act of having her back against its impenetrable weight would be enough to protect her if the wolf charged. Then she angled herself, putting Jacob between her and the steel as if she could ward off danger if the wolf tried to get through her to him. Her neck turned as far as it could possibly turn, keeping the wolf in sight.

It moved, gliding like a fish darting in and out of water through that front line of trees, slinking parallel to her progress. Then she was up by the headlights, and there was nothing left to cling to; there was only the empty expanse between her and the front door.

"Go. Don't run, just go. Keep eye contact," Chaz rapid-fired instructions. "Don't turn your back. He can't think you're prey."

But she was prey. She knew it, so the wolf must surely have known it. She was nothing but a puffy winter coat over a regular body, a body made of blood and meat and bones just like the body of any other creature this wolf might hunt down. And she was holding another body that was even more tender still.

She kept eye contact with the wolf as if their two gazes were connected by an invisible wire. Its eyes were a pale yellow-green that flashed into mirrors each time they caught the beam of the headlights. She walked on a strange angle, not really seeing where she was going, until she slipped over the rocks, almost falling. The wolf took a half-step forward.

"He's just waiting for you guys to give him a reason," Chaz said.

Then they gave him one.

Jacob, as if alert to her anxiety, snapped his eyes fully open. He looked around and felt lost. He breathed frigid air into his sensitive lungs and let out a long, piercing wail. Eleni's gaze went down to him as he flailed his arms, like the helpless prey he was, and the wolf started from the trees.

He was quick and gray over white snow. Eleni saw him coming and reflexively bolted to the stairs, tripping on the first one and banging Jacob's back on the porch. His wails grew louder, and Eleni screamed. Chaz was mumbling, fumbling. A shot went off, stunning Jacob into silence. Then Eleni felt the quick, hot breath of the wolf against her leg, which was sticking out behind her after her awkward fall.

A second shot.

The yelp of a dog.

Eleni clutched Jacob, both of them trembling, both hysterical. Her eardrums throbbed painfully from the shots. Crimson blood stained the white snow.

The wolf dragged himself away after being shot, coming to rest near the tree line. His hip was shattered by the bullet, and he was bleeding out. His breath continued, slower but steady, plume after plume as he stared off into the woods and his back feet twitched.

The blood on the snow reminded her of flowers: huge, exploding carnations.

Chaz reloaded the gun.

"Told you I had you," he said, unnerved but proud. Eleni got to her feet, shaking; Jacob was now crying in earnest. She scooped him up and, somehow, made it up the steps without falling.

She turned at the top of the stairs and nodded at Chaz, backing herself up to the door, wanting to be inside, wanting it to be over.

"Thank you," she managed to get out, voice breaking. "Thank you, Chaz."

"That's my job. I'm good at it." He smiled. Eleni's vision blurred and her legs grew numb.

"You sure you're gonna be all right now?"

Eleni nodded, despite a voice in her head screaming, *No, absolutely not. Get back in the truck. Just leave the luggage. Get the hell out of here.*

But she heard herself saying, "The worst is over."

Chaz nodded, eyes still sweeping the woods to make sure no other wolves were going to come out. The shots seemed to have scared them off. Eleni wondered if people heard them in town.

"You'll be back to check in tomorrow, right? No matter what?" Eleni asked.

"Sure. Tomorrow or day after."

Please come tomorrow, she thought, but she nodded.

"You'll be fine. Just don't set foot outside. You got food enough for a week. Once Ben's here, you'll have nothing to worry about."

She kept on nodding, then pushed against the door with her back, still jittery, casting a glance over to the dying, bleeding wolf one last time. His tongue hung out, long and languid, dripping saliva in one intact stream. The door squeaked open against the door frame.

"Thank you, Chaz. Drive safe."

She stepped back inside, quickly shutting the door, imagining wolves everywhere. In her imagination, running parallel to the actual moment, they somehow appeared faster than the speed of light to wedge themselves in the door before she could close it. She shoved the door fully closed and locked it, then slid the extra deadbolt home.

She went to the window, placing Jacob on the bed beneath it. His cries had dulled down to little hitches in his breathing. She kept an arm around him, and they stared out together.

Chaz lowered himself back down through the moon roof. Snowflakes swirled in the two horizontal cones of light from his headlights. His windshield wipers groaned back to life, screeching over an accumulated layer of white.

He waited a minute or two. She knew he could see their faces, still registering the shock of the wolf encounter, staring out from behind the barred window. She thought about waving her arms, signaling for him to wait. They could still leave.

But she didn't. Somehow, it would have seemed more than just cowardly. It would have seemed impolite, as if she didn't care about seeing Ben.

The pact they'd made during that far-off summer was to each put the other first, no matter how crazy, no matter what else it cost them. It was never overtly spoken, but something they'd gradually come into through shared experiences and displays of love that, while they at first seemed strange, gradually were offered up as proof that Ben was fully in this. She needed to be fully in it too. If she broke this pact, it would be like she wasn't worthy of his love. Maybe like she wasn't capable of loving in the full-out, real way he had taught her to love.

Her hand started, for only an instant, as if to rise and signal Chaz . . . but it only jumped forward an inch or two on the windowsill.

"Mommy, don't like it," Jacob said between hiccups. "I don't like it, Mommy."

She stroked his head, which was covered with a thick wool hat.

"It'll be ok, baby. We'll make the best of it."

"No, Mommy, don't like it," and he was crying again.

As Jacob sobbed, she watched Chaz put the truck into gear, drive in an arc closer to the cabin, and turn around. She saw his faint outline in the cab, giving her a sharp, perfunctory half-wave goodbye over the steering wheel. Somehow, it felt like the cries she heard came from her own throat.

But she couldn't leave now.

The truck left heavy tracks in the snow. It somehow, mysteriously, picked its way back into the woods, the branches closing over it. The red of the tail lights glowed from inside the pines for a few moments, then he was gone.

4

SETTLING IN

She kept Jacob in his full winter regalia for a while, holding him long and tight while she waited for the adrenaline-induced jitters to leave her body. It was frigid in the cabin, despite the space heaters. As his crying petered out, she pointed to their hypnotic glow and warned him not to touch. He stared at her, his mouth agape. He was good at listening to warnings.

She knelt in front of the fireplace, checking if the flue was open. It was. The wind howled down the vertical, stone corridor of the chimney. She pulled off her mittens, placing them on the brick ledge that held the woodpile, and stuck a hand into the fireplace's black mouth, feeling the night air prick down at her. She put a store-bought "instant" log in the center of the hearth.

Jacob stayed on the bed, still peering out the window, searching for more wolves. Right when it seemed he would turn away and look for some other kind of amusement, a long, plaintive howl came from somewhere beyond the trees.

She remembered watching a documentary once about wolves mourning their dead. If a mate was killed, the one left behind would howl like that.

Eleni, who had picked through the pile of small, chopped logs and was stacking a few in the fireplace, stopped. Jacob turned fully to the glass, now on his knees, looking out.

"You see anything, baby?" she asked, trying to sound casual, like it was all a game. She tucked the small hand axe propped up by the woodpile behind it to keep it out of Jacob's sight.

"All dark," he said. It was less in answer to her question than it was a surprised announcement. She supposed he'd never seen such complete, total darkness before. Their studio back home was downtown; street lamps hung just outside their windows, and even when their curtains closed at bedtime, the rooms were coated in pale light.

"We're out in the woods," she told him, wondering if the past few days' worth of her saying, "We're taking a trip to the woods . . . having an adventure in the woods . . ." had registered at all. Even if they had, he had no frame of reference for what "woods" meant. It was all new to him, and it would all have been unexpected, no matter what "it" turned out to be.

She was just glad his tears had calmed and that they hadn't brought on any other attacks.

"Woods," he repeated, still looking. He sat and turned to see her, right as she fished a large box of matches out from behind the woodpile. The springs creaked slightly beneath him. "Mean doggie, Mommy."

"It was a wolf," she said, striking a match. Tears crowded her vision as she held the flame to the paper wrapper of the starter log until it caught. Thank God she hadn't had to start the fire from scratch.

She blew the match out and swatted at her eyes. Jacob, referring to the match smell and connecting it to candles on a cake, said, "It smells like birthday," and she pulled the rusty iron screen over the fire.

"Can wolfs get in, Mommy?"

She shook her head, still facing away from him. "No. They can't get in."

26

Not unless we let them.

It wasn't the first time she'd been struck by how much her son relied on her for total protection. Even on the flight from Seattle to Juneau, she'd had a moment right before the plane took off where it seemed downright unfair that this small boy had to do whatever she said. She'd looked at him, buckled into his airplane seat and staring out at the tarmac as the doors closed with a heavy, clunking *swoosh*. He was on the plane. He had no say in the matter. If the plane went down, he'd go down with it; there'd be no choice. And he wouldn't have had any say in it whatsoever.

She stood, picking up her mittens, and walked to the small dining table to deposit them there. Her hair crackled slightly from static as she pulled her hat off. It started to feel marginally warmer in the cabin.

"Do you want a snack?" she asked.

"Want Cute-lings," he said, and she half-smiled. He loved the Cute-lings, a show they found online that consisted of talking toys fashioned by stay-at-home parents trying to become YouTube celebrities. But there was no Internet access here, of course. Only a few episodes of more polished, studio kids' shows she'd downloaded to her phone.

She set him up watching one, pulling off his hat and smoothing his fine, brown hair. A short while later, it was comfortable enough inside to pull off his heavy winter coat, small boots, and snowsuit. He soon shed all his extra layers and was down to his red fleece outfit—pajamas that could double as play clothes—with a moose embroidered on the front and red-and-black-checked pants.

There were no drawers or closets to put anything away, so she piled his winter gear on the table in the far corner. In the past, she'd kept a suitcase under the bed for her clothes.

"I'm going to put the food away," she said. Entranced by his show full of talking trains, he barely noticed her anymore. In the kitchen, she went through the bags of groceries. Dried beans, granola bars, cans of soup, boxes of uncooked couscous, raisins, and cookies went into the cupboards and along the counter. Eggs, milk, juice, and smoked salmon—lots of it—went into the fridge.

In one of the bags was a plastic toy truck she'd also gotten at the store, to get Jacob a prize. He'd since forgotten about it. Out in the living room, she heard Jacob say to himself, "Daddy's coming," speaking the thought aloud as it ran through his head.

An icy cold ran up the side of her leg, the one facing the door to the "basement." The way Ben had built the cabin, on a slight hill, there was a small dug-out area they'd always referred to as the "basement," despite the fact it had walls and a floor made of dirt and was really more a small, back section of the house. The door in the kitchen opened to only six wooden planks descending down, set into the earth. Down below was the backup generator (the main one was outside, beside the house), an ancient wringer for laundry, and two slanted cellar doors up an incline, which could open wide and lead into the woods.

Somewhere right beyond those doors was a well-worn path, leading to the fjord and a small dock Ben had built, where he used to keep his seaplane. He taught her (illegally, she was pretty sure) how to fly it that summer, with the odd lesson out on the water the only thing to occupy their time besides making love or playing cards. Thinking about how she'd made the plane go erratically up and down gave her stomach the floating, tickling sensation of plunging down a large hill on a roller coaster. She wondered if that was how he'd arrive tonight.

It was entirely possible that Ben left one or both of those weathered cellar doors open. He did it at least once before, back when they lived here. An adolescent moose managed to stumble in and had kicked its hooves deep into the dirt walls before it figured out how to escape. She and Ben heard the commotion and waited, listening through the basement door, unsure exactly which creature had gotten inside. Later, they'd gone down the steps to survey the damage, Ben holding his gun and Eleni behind his outstretched arm. She'd traced her fingers in the hoof prints rutted into the rocky earth and repacked old crates that were kicked over, spilling their contents.

Chaz would have just gotten the outside generator up and running today. He wouldn't have checked the basement. The door might literally have been open for years; anything could be down there.

She lingered a moment, sensing the cold through her thick clothes. The basement door was just plywood painted white, with a small barrel slide lock screwed into the wall. It was flimsy.

It occurred to her that she should maybe check whether the outer doors were closed and not flung open to the wilderness. She should make sure they were as secure as possible, but she knew there was no way she would do it. Not with the wolves.

She pushed the thick block of a wooden table in front of the door, even though the door could still be reduced to splinters, and, hesitatingly, turned back to the living area.

It was nice to curl up with Jacob in front of the fire and watch him grow drowsy and try to fight against the closing of his eyes. At one point, he focused on her face, touched her cheeks, and said, "Best Mommy."

Her heart sang, and she kissed his forehead. It didn't stop the sense of dread that was coming on, though. She wasn't at all sure she was even a good mommy, let alone the best one. After all . . . she'd put him on that plane this morning.

5

THAT SUMMER

Jacob was out cold. They lay on the bed, facing the fire, with Eleni curled around him. She felt the rise and fall of his breathing against her. Every so often, she lifted her head just to look down at him and appreciate the beauty of his face.

The bed had been dusty. Before they'd officially climbed under the blanket, she'd taken it off to shake it out over the old tub in the bathroom. She didn't want the dust aggravating Jacob's asthma; part of her was surprised it hadn't already.

The cabin had warmed up better than she'd expected. It was still cool in the kitchen, but here, under the oppressively heavy quilt, in front of the fire, the space heater humming just a few feet away, they were cozy. They'd kept their socks on, though, and she had a heavy sweatshirt on over her long-sleeve t-shirt and tank top, both part of the dark green-and-plaid pajama set she wore. She'd gotten the sweatshirt that summer with Ben and put it on in a fit of nostalgia when deciding to make this trip. It was maroon with black trim and a small, embroidered black bear hovering over her heart. The word *"Alaska"* was scrawled in thread beneath the bear. Ben bought it for her on a weekend getaway to an obscure tourist town whose only claim to fame was a massive collection of taxidermied animals from the Yukon.

31

She'd never been a snappy dresser, and her hair even now was pulled back haphazardly with an elastic bought in a convenience store. Especially since having Jacob and losing Ben, sweats and ponytails had been her look of choice. The consistency with which she wore sweats wasn't something she consciously thought about, but every time she pulled open her drawers, she automatically reached for the same outfits over and over again. Soft and oversized, they were things she could more or less hide inside, the elastic waistband of the pants always pulled up above her belly button to protect a stomach that, while not necessarily flabby, had lost all its tone in the wake of having a child. In a weird way, the clothes weren't only chosen to protect her from other people's roving eyes but also to protect Ben from having other people look at her, protect them both from her having to make any kind of a choice should someone become interested in her.

She held Jacob close and stared at the fire, still going strong. How many fires had she enjoyed inside this cabin? How many times had she lain on this bed? She opened the hand that was resting in front of Jacob and ran it over the surface of the quilt. This was where Jacob had been conceived.

The day that Ben had run, she hadn't yet known she was pregnant. When she found out, she'd told Chaz on the off chance Ben would be "in touch" with him. Chaz leered at her as if this information somehow invited him into their intimate relationship. It somehow seemed to make her into even more of an object than before.

Later, when the cops came to question her (which they did for months), she had, of course, told them too. She thought about lying and saying the baby wasn't Ben's. It felt almost like she'd put bad luck on the child by acknowledging his father was hiding from the law. She'd never been good at lying, though. Luckily, they didn't hold her, and they didn't forbid her to leave Alaska. They'd let her move back home to have the baby.

She'd fought to go home but found little support there. The reason she'd come back—the pregnancy—was the very reason she was ostracized from what family she had. Any disconnect she felt from Jacob when he was a newborn—the entire experience surreal, his sudden existence disorienting—soon evaporated as she dove ever-more into being a mother, not only because of instinct but because she really had nothing else left in her life.

It was strange, now, to be back in a place so charged with memories from before she became a mom. It felt like no time had passed at all; it was as if the thing with the police, with Aimee Hart, had only been a bad dream, and they'd simply never left that summer.

Ben had been the first true romance of her life.

Every other relationship had always felt forced. She wanted a boyfriend, so she convinced herself she liked the men that came into her life. They wanted a girlfriend, and she was suitable enough. There'd never been any real connection, though, nothing like you saw in movies or read about in books.

It was different with Ben, though.

The first time she'd seen him, he was sitting on a wooden fence right outside the tour guide office. The building's façade was done to look like something out of the Old West, the actual office only a small square room hanging off the back of it. It was down the street from the railway depot where they'd both be working during the summer.

Ben was handsome, casual, chatting with one of his friends . . . a manager of the tour place, who'd picked her up at the ferry and drove her to the office, pulled into the gravel lot just in front of him. Ben looked up and smiled. Never before, in the whole rest of her life, had anyone she thought was handsome actually become interested in her too. It was as if they could sense she found them attractive, and it actively repelled them. But not Ben.

She wasn't skilled at talking to new people. Being a tour guide was different; she had a script and could follow jokes that had been tested over time. She'd enjoyed being in plays back in high school, too, always in small, supporting roles, and this felt like the same kind of thing. But in one-on-one conversation, she seized up, throat tight, scared of saying or doing something wrong. He chatted with her easily, though, as if he didn't realize how quiet she was or how her main talent was only to politely smile and feign interest. (Not that it was feigned with him.) He leaned into her and touched her arm while the bald eagles circled overhead.

That night, the sun still dimly out at 10 p.m., the managers threw a summer kick-off party on the large expanse of stones by the river. There was a bonfire, and bottles of straight, hard liquor were passed around. One of the other tour guides, Paul, propped a large chest of gold rush costumes up on a bench. They'd all be wearing them that summer when they gave their tours, and they tried on goofy hats and fur stoles, getting their pictures taken, toasting the Yukon. She'd been in some pictures but wasn't boisterous like a lot of the others. One girl in particular, Janine, with striking long, black hair and perfect nails that reminded Eleni of the girls in Hallmark movies, had been the type to dominate every conversation.

After the distraction of the costumes, Eleni slowly migrated back to the outskirts of the crowd, watching the fire. She didn't drink from any of the communal bottles.

She noticed him, of course, that guy who had talked with her earlier, that handsome guy who seemed to get along with everyone and who Janine kept calling on for conversation. Eleni didn't dare approach him. It wasn't that she didn't think she had things to offer. It was just that she didn't think she could convince anyone else she had them.

Things were winding down, and she was sitting, uncomfortably, on a log by the fire when he sat down next to her.

"Well, since it looks like you're going to go all night without speaking to me, figured I finally had to give in and come to you," he said, smiling and extending a bottle of vodka.

"Oh," she said, out of sheer surprise, then laughed nervously. He was a charmer, for sure. She begged herself to come up with some clever retort and managed "didn't want to interrupt," nodding toward the dissipating throng of other tour guides, including Janine, who was now watching them and looking slightly crestfallen.

"It would've been welcome," he said, waggling the bottle at her again. She took it to be polite but only held it in her lap. He looked at her in a way that told her he noted this fact.

"So, you're kind of shy," he said, completely in control of everything, only seconds into the conversation. She shrugged.

"What can I say?"

"No. I like that about you."

She beamed at him then, feeling acknowledged. The curse of shyness had suddenly transformed into a blessing, just like that, because Ben Wilton liked it about her.

"Makes one of us," she said, happy with her response. She sounded a little clever, after all.

"Really. It's so much more special than the girls who just talk, talk, talk." *Girls like Janine*, Eleni thought. Deep down, without even realizing it, she made a mental note not to be one of those girls. "The ones who are all about getting attention."

"I think I avoid attention," she said, suddenly trying to prove herself. *I can be just what you want me to be.*

"I could tell the moment I met you," he said, fixating on her with his clear, blue eyes. "You're something special."

She lifted the bottle to her lips and drank.

She had never been pursued before. Not really. She'd been asked out a couple of times by a few shy and embarrassed guys who wouldn't have been all that hurt if she said no. But with Ben, it had been an active, decided pursuit.

He sought her out. Each tour guide had been given lodging in a small, six-by-eight-foot cabin that consisted solely of a space heater, cot, and chest of drawers. No plumbing, one bare lightbulb overhead. He would show up to walk her to the train depot at the start of the day and leave notes tacked on her front door asking her to come hang out in the small kitchen in the main building, where the one bathroom and shower also were. He would invite her on hikes with the rest of the group when the others had seemingly forgotten about her and to his living space to show her pictures and listen to music and drink. He bought her a necklace in town—a small leaf that had been bronzed and turned into a pendant—and insisted she wear it all the time, even under her old-time tour guide outfit. (She caught hell later when, at the end of a long day, she lifted a hand to her throat and found it was gone.)

He told her all about his almost-completed cabin two miles beyond town limits, which could only be reached by following "animal roads"—the narrow, practically non-existent pathways forged by bears and wolves making their way through the woods. Over the course of two years, he'd built it himself, and it was now, finally, almost ready to be lived in. He'd even rigged actual plumbing from a well he and his friends dug and set up a composting toilet. There was electricity, thanks to generators. He beamed with pride whenever he spoke of it, and she was full of admiration and envy for someone who could create something like that with his own two hands.

He would take her there one day.

The actual moment when she became "Ben's girlfriend" was unclear. She knew he liked her because of all the attention, but she was afraid she'd so much as breathe and wreck it. It felt so fragile, so beyond what her actual reality had been up to that point. No one had ever set their sights on her. There'd never oeen this kind of adventure—the quiet, internal adventure of budding romance, where every conversation felt legendary.

He never officially asked her to be his girlfriend. Instead, all of a sudden, he just began talking about her like she was "his." He just began kissing her as they sat in his cabin, listening to music, leaning in and doing it while she was still smiling over something else. With Eleni unaware of what was coming, his lips momentarily caught on her teeth.

His kiss was hard, forceful, in a way that made her jaw ache, but she was so grateful for it she didn't mind.

He introduced her to someone as his girlfriend, and she beamed with pride. Janine glared at her from the sidelines. She'd never been the girl another girl was jealous of before, and the fact that Janine was now jealous contained its own private layers of validation. What's more, other people took more note of her. Other girls confided about how jealous Janine was, while Eleni got to be magnanimous in shrugging it off.

Part of her felt that maybe this was a new era in her life. Perhaps it was time to be the kind of person she could only have fantasized about being before, one who would be the object of this much attention and romance.

Unexpectedly, though, being that person also meant she opened herself to more scrutiny. In the past, she'd flown under the radar, but it now felt like she had a neon target on her back. On one occasion, when she went to get her laundry out of the communal machines in the main building, Eleni had found Janine sitting beside a pile of Eleni's clothes, which had been pulled out of the dryer and dumped on the table. Two other girls, Janine's friends, sat nearby. Janine was holding up one of Eleni's tank tops by its spaghetti strap, staring at it like a rat being held by its tail. Eleni only caught " . . . little dishrag . . ." but could safely assume from the way the conversation cut off that Janine had been talking about her. Janine's face turned pink, and she allowed Eleni to snatch the item from her hand. Eleni murmured, "That's my stuff," but all three of them remained silent. There was no excuse-making, no apologies. Eleni simply gathered her clothes into her arms and walked out, hearing nasty laughter behind her as the door closed. It was the laughter of people who knew they were in the wrong but who would cover it up with insulting jokes and reverie.

Things like that made her avoid other people even more and grow ever more consumed by Ben. Hearing the stories, he further encouraged her devotion to him, telling her to always have him with her when she did her laundry and not to hang out in the break room without him either.

Janine had proven herself prone to drama. When she went on a hike, she twisted her ankle and needed to be carried back by two guys (although the same ankle was fine when it was time to go out later that night). She felt the need to talk loudly about her exploits in town, sharing details about the guys who hit on her and the drunk girls who spilled their drinks on her shoes. For those not in her circle, she quickly latched on to small details about them she disliked, then blew them up to epic proportions, her entire social life based around the mocking of others. She was the type that, once interested in someone, was relentless about getting their attention—and she tried to get Ben's on a daily basis. But Ben was with Eleni, whether Janine liked it or not.

Ben's love was intense. He talked about their being together in whole, complete terms, right from those early days. She knew that if Tiff had been around, it would have set off red flags for her. But then she thought that perhaps Tiff—and everyone else she knew—simply never experienced such deep, true love themselves. Love was what it had to be.

It hadn't been more than a few days since he'd started addressing her as his girlfriend that he told her, "I know protocol. I know people should date for a year before they make any big moves—but I'll tell ya, I could buy the ring right now."

So many things in her life that seemed practical to expect, but also as if they could never really happen—things like getting married—suddenly seemed startlingly close, and the effect was dizzying, joyful. She walked around with giddy excitement over everything she suddenly had and everything it seemed she *would* have—being the girlfriend of someone so handsome and charming, being a bride, being a mother. Ben talked, off-hand, about how he could tell she'd make such a great mother.

The first time they slept together, they'd only known each other a few weeks. While that might be more than enough for some people, for Eleni, who had only been with two other people, that was moving pretty fast. With past boyfriends, she'd gone on a months-long series of unspectacular dates before building to a time when it felt like she either needed to sleep with them or accept that the relationship should end. Her first time had been brief and painful, and she'd walked around the next day feeling like there was a deep bruise between her legs that someone kept pressing. Sex wasn't something other partners discussed in too much detail before those lackluster trysts, aside from the discussion of using protection.

Ben, though, talked about sex all the time. He talked about how irresistible she was, about how it was all he could think about. No one had ever talked to her like that before. She'd never felt like an object of desire. She wasn't a super smart girl, but it did occur to her to wonder, later, in the stretch of three-plus years after Ben had gone and she was left with time and space to think (not to mention a baby that looked vaguely like him), whether she had really felt about him as passionately as she thought she did—or if part of her passionate feelings were just the thrill of seeing herself the way he claimed to see her. She fell in love with him, but she really fell in love with herself as an object of passion and desire.

"So, what's it gonna take?" he asked her one night, lying beside her on her cot, lazy, trailing his fingers up and down her bare arm.

She shrugged. "I mean, I just want it to be special."

"Won't it be special?" He looked at her meaningfully. "Because it's us."

"Of course, but you know . . . like romantic."

"You don't think I can be romantic?"

She held him off for about a week, making excuses about needing things to be "just right." Nerves consumed her. She was afraid that when they finally slept together, he would see she wasn't as spectacular or sexy as he'd originally thought. But then, at the end of the week, she'd gone over to hang out, and he'd lit candles and gotten flowers and had on beautiful music . . . all things she'd mentioned as possible contributors to the "perfect night" in an earlier conversation. It was so clear he'd gotten all these things because she said she wanted them for their first time that she felt it needed to be then.

She let him take her clothes off, and she heard some of the other tour guides talking outside as they walked by, right beyond the thin walls. It felt as if they were inside with them. Ratty, worn curtains were drawn over the one square window, but Eleni was worried people could peek around the corners. She heard Janine's sharp, barking laughter at some point, and it was enough to make her entire body tense up.

"Say that you're mine," Ben had said, laying her down on the bed. She'd laughed nervously. Sometimes, the grand pronouncements, the requests for over-the-top declarations, felt silly. They were things people said in movies, not in real life.

But didn't everyone want a movie kind of love?

"Say it," he prompted again, smiling, lying down on top of her. Skin on skin.

"I'm yours," she said. Then, in a burst of inspiration, "I'm completely yours."

And he was in.

—⚏—

He'd wanted to have sex every day, sometimes more than once a day. There was almost a hysteria about it, the need for it to be obsessive and all-consuming. It was impossible for her to put it off. When they did go, one night, to a social gathering including more than only the two of them, he got moody and restless when she talked to James, another tour guide.

That night, there was a barrage of questions about what exactly she thought was and wasn't appropriate in terms of her having "male friends." Would she go to coffee with a male friend? Hang out in one's cabin? How much did she talk with them during work? Did she realize they probably wanted to sleep with her?

The whole thing led to a tense conversation, the first in their relationship. He told her about a past girlfriend he'd loved who cheated on him. He apologized but said he just needed a lot of reassurance that she was faithful. She comforted him and felt terrible about his past experience. It was like the time she'd tried to prove she wasn't an attention seeker in order to please him; only this time, she had to prove exactly how loyal she was. In the coming weeks, this new responsibility would manifest itself in cutting off any conversations with male co-workers and sitting alone at lunch.

In bed again after their initial, tense talk, Eleni now sharing his small, twin-sized cot almost every night, he said, "This is how we're best. Just the two of us. We should just do this all the time."

Not long after that, his cabin was fully done, and Ben suggested they go there for the rest of the summer.

"Just quit this job," he said. "It sucks, anyway. I can get another job, out with the horseback riding? It pays better, and you wouldn't have to do a thing, just relax and enjoy it."

"I can't just sit around doing nothing."

"Why not? That's your parents talking, not you. Just relax. Let me take care of you like I want to."

They'd barely spoken of her parents. He had only a vague sense of two people, rigid in their beliefs, standing as steady, constantly disappointed figures in the background of her life.

He kissed her and talked on about how it would be, the two of them, in this perfect little heaven he'd assembled from logs and cement. It was a corner of the world that he'd perfected for himself, never knowing that he'd find someone he'd want to share it with. He was now so, so grateful that he had.

She wouldn't be able to get back and forth from the cabin to work. It wouldn't be possible to get through the complicated, wooded path on her own. She'd have to quit.

Since they'd gotten together, Ben withdrew more and more from the people they worked with, finding fault with them in one way or another. Almost nightly, he'd tell her some horror story about this one or that, whittling down the number of people that it was "acceptable" to hang out with even further. Feeling wronged became the norm, and when he told stories of things done to him during the day, Eleni had to agree they sounded awful. One of the other guides had taken their guests onto a numbered train car that was supposed to be Ben's, leaving his group stranded until a new assignment could be made. His wallet went missing, and even though it turned up later, he insisted it was $20 short of what it had been. When the kitchen gave him his daily bag of lunches for the tourists one day, they shorted him on the lunch that was supposed to have been his, meaning he had to go without. This happened to Eleni once, too, and she genuinely believed the kitchen staff when she sheepishly brought it up; they made over 300 of these lunches a day, and sometimes mistakes happened. But Ben was fed up with that place and ready for something new, something better. Something for only them.

One night, shortly before making the decision to leave, Eleni found herself in a rare moment without Ben, in her room. Janine knocked on the door. Her eyes were puffy, like she'd been crying. Eleni was stunned to see her and quickly glanced up and down the wooden plank walkway that connected the cabins, looking for Ben for protection. One of Janine's friends, a girl who'd also been in the laundry room on that day, stood about fifteen feet away, arms crossed, an acting security blanket for Janine. Eleni almost asked Janine if Ben was who she was actually there to see.

"Hey," Janine sniffed, looking over Eleni's shoulder, checking to see if Ben was concealed inside. "Got a minute?"

Eleni shrugged, completely off-guard. Janine looked at the ground, gave a wet, sloppy sniff, and wiped her nose with the back of her hand. Eleni didn't know if Janine expected her to start, but then she had no idea what the conversation was about.

"So, I know you and I haven't really gotten along," Janine finally said, still looking at the ground. "I haven't really been fair to you."

Eleni kept staring, the cool outside air beginning to negate the steady effort of her space heater, just inside.

"You and Ben, you're like, together," Janine said. Everyone knew that. Eleni kept waiting. "Like, I knew you were together, and I still fooled around with him. I'm sorry. I am."

Janine began to talk more quickly, in a panic, as if she expected Eleni to jump all over her after the revelation of her "fooling around." But Eleni was just quiet, just watching.

"I should never have done that because it was wrong, wrong to you, but, you know, I liked him, and I was just a bitch, and I'm sorry . . ."

Eleni furrowed her brow and shifted her weight from one foot to the other.

"But I'm telling you now because . . ." Janine trailed off, her voice slowing down again now that she saw Eleni was going to let her get it all out. She took a deep breath. "He was being a dick. And I told him I was going to tell you. And he got so mad, and he—pushed me. Like, kind of a weird push, sideways, so I'd hit the drawers. He said he'd tripped. But he threatened me, told me he'd kill me if I told you."

She met Eleni's eyes, her own eyes huge and blue, the whites gone pink in her smooth, cream-colored face. She pulled up the side of her sweatshirt and showed Eleni some faint, almost non-existent purple bruising along her bottom rib as if that proved it.

Eleni looked up and down the path again, looking for Ben. It felt like a betrayal to him to be having this conversation now. Janine's friend looked solemn, as if standing there for this was the most important duty a friend could ever fulfill.

"I don't think he's safe. And I know I'm making a fool of myself, but I wouldn't have felt ok not letting you know that."

But you felt ok screwing him behind my back?

Janine was done, the whole story now told, however ineloquently. Eleni finally spoke because it was undeniably her turn to do so.

"Thank you for telling me."

Her voice sounded sincere enough. She backed up into her small single room, refusing to meet Janine's eye.

"Yeah," Janine said, backing up too. Eleni almost asked if she'd told the police, but then she didn't want to give Janine any ideas. Who knew what a drama queen would do when scorned, and Eleni told herself she didn't believe the story. She'd slept with Ben now; they were bonded. Janine had done nothing but make her uncomfortable since she arrived.

Janine turned and disappeared down the wooden walkway. It was the last time they spoke.

—ɱ—

Eleni remembered the first ride out to the cabin with Ben, after quitting, her one suitcase in the back of his truck. She'd squealed going over the old Gold Rush Bridge, not out of genuine fear of plunging down into the river but with the excitement and adventure of it all. She squirmed in her seat, holding Ben's hand.

They'd picked their way down the "animal trail," through the trees, but it hadn't felt harrowing. It felt like entering someplace enchanted, a secret world out of a fairy tale. It was like the branches magically parted for them, the sun beating down into the green to create a bright, welcoming light, permeating the brilliant summer colors of the forest. When they came carefully out on the ledge above the fjord, she hadn't noticed that they were flirting with the edge of a cliff so much as she had how the sun sparkled off the water, majestic and regal mountains bordering this scene on all sides. Otters splashed down below, and knowing there were also orcas, she watched to see if she could spot one.

She was living an actual life, an adventurous life.

When the cabin suddenly revealed itself, it was spellbinding. The sun beat down on it, and it was perfect, its wood new and polished, the door freshly painted maroon. Its porch roof was sturdy and attractive. Even the bars on the windows weren't off-putting; she hardly noticed them at first glance.

"Wait," Ben said, holding a hand up to keep her in her seat. He ran around to her side, lifted her out, and carried her up the porch steps, laughing, and over the threshold into their new life. He put her on the bed for the very first time, and it felt luxurious to be on something larger than the small cot back at work, where the managers were still stewing over her sudden resignation.

"Eleni," Laurie, the one manager who perpetually wore a yellow rain slicker, had said, "think about what you're doing. You really want to do this?"

Eleni had nodded, wanting the end result but hating having to go through the conversation.

"But this wasn't your idea. Going off alone into the woods? I mean, you really think that's a good idea?"

Eleni had nodded again. "We're just . . . we're ready to have our own place."

Laurie had sighed, rubbed her forehead. "I wish you would reconsider."

As far as Eleni knew, Ben hadn't gotten the same kind of talk. From what she heard, he had quit, and they'd simply asked him to turn in the key to his cabin. But with her, they tried to persuade her to stay.

"They know you're an easier mark," Ben said, stroking her hair affectionately. "Soft touch."

"Well, they didn't break me," she joked. He kissed her. It was like a reward, a continual reward system to do anything that pleased him and supported him. Like a dog being thrown treats, she was thrown kisses, touches, compliments . . .

You are worth something.

She never told him the last thing Laurie said, though, which even though Eleni resisted it, she knew would cause friction if repeated out loud. Ben would doubt her loyalty, just for repeating it.

Laurie dropped her hands onto her desk, tented over her clipboard, almost as if begging.

"Eleni," she said again, past the point of dropping mere hints, "please, please don't go off with this person."

Eleni, still sitting awkwardly on the folding chair in the office, was genuinely confused. "What do you mean?"

"It's not my place," Laurie said in a quick, perfunctory way. As if saying that made it ok to say what came next. "I just don't think this is a good idea for you."

Eleni was stunned. Other people did things like this. They fell in love, moved in together. There was a big turnover in jobs like this; it might be frustrating for the managers, but it was just how it was. The workers were from all over, wanting an Alaskan adventure. Eleni herself, with her strained family relationships back home, had seen a flyer on a corkboard at a grocery store in Washington and decided she had nothing to lose. This wasn't anyone's long-term career. It was a summer escape.

"Well, I am going, so . . ." Eleni trailed off but forced herself to maintain eye contact with Laurie.

"You don't have to, though," Laurie said, not blinking.

Eleni looked down. She broke eye contact first. "But I am. It's already decided."

"You're allowed to change your mind."

Truth be told, Eleni wasn't exactly sure when she had decided on this; it was sort of like becoming Ben's girlfriend. All of a sudden, he called her his girlfriend. With the move to the woods, one moment it was a hypothetical conversation, and the next, he was talking to her like it had been their definite plan all along, asking her when she was going to give her notice.

It was like that joke about salesmen and how they never asked whether or not you actually wanted to buy what they were selling. They only asked if you wanted it in red or blue.

She didn't know when she'd decided, but somewhere along the way she must have, because here she was now.

"I don't want to change my mind. It's made up."

Laurie had nodded, sadness creeping across her face.

"Is this because of what Janine's been saying?" Eleni asked.

"Janine has nothing to do with it."

"Then?"

Laurie sighed, scratched her forehead, and looked away.

"Look, I said what I needed to. I hope you'll be in touch if you need anything at all."

She hadn't really said what she needed to, though. Unspoken was what she really thought of Ben, after just the month or so that they'd all worked together. She left that to Eleni's imagination.

But Eleni, once inside the cabin, like a magical cottage in a story, hadn't had to think about the managers at all anymore. They were back in town, two miles through the woods. It might as well have been two hundred. She was in a different world out here.

The first time they made love in the cabin, sunlight streamed through the front window, down onto the bed, onto their backs and arms and legs and torsos. There was no fear about anyone seeing them, about any fellow workers walking by and hearing them through the thin walls. No fear about gossip or laughter. Eleni looked up at the slanting rays of sun with tears in her eyes because she was so happy, feeling like she'd finally come home even though home was the middle of nowhere. Her tears blurred her vision and created prismatic rainbows in the sunlight, and she couldn't tell where she ended and where Ben began.

Eleni's eyes snapped open. In an instant, she went from the green, sun-drenched scene of lying in Ben's arms to blackness, lit only with dull oranges and reds from the fireplace. She had fallen asleep and stepped back three and a half years; now, here she was again, and she had to walk herself through the past months to remember all that had happened.

She had a son. Ben's son. He was sleeping, pressed against her.

Ben had been gone for over three years.

He was wanted for murder.

She sat up and looked around, now back in the cabin. Though she was fully back, it felt like an entirely different place . . . or, more disconcertingly, like a veil had been lifted off the place where she'd been, revealing it was nothing like she'd actually believed.

What had woken her up? There had been a noise, a sputter. She looked around, and it took a moment for her to realize the space heater had shut off.

She climbed off the bed and looked at the space heater in the dining area. That was off, too, so this wasn't a case of just one going bad.

The generator must have gone out.

The cold was already seeping back in, lacing its way through the toasty air.

"Sometimes you have to reset it," Ben told her once as he showed her how.

"Crap," she hissed, pacing, wondering exactly what time it was. She dug her cell phone from her backpack, able to check the time even if it didn't have any service. 12:01 a.m. Who knew when Ben would get here? She couldn't let Jacob sleep all night in the freezing cold, and it would only get worse with each passing moment.

She paced into the kitchen, stood in front of the somewhat-barricaded basement door, and again felt the frigid air leaking from the crack at the bottom, pooling around her feet in their thick wool socks.

The doors in the basement might be fully open, exposed to the woods.

She had to go down.

6

THE DEN

Eleni pulled her thick parka on over her pajamas, wrapped her scarf around her neck, and slipped back into her heavy snow boots.

She left Jacob lying on the bed, tucking the blanket firmly beneath his chin. He inhaled and exhaled deeply, turning onto his back and casting his arm out to the side. The light from the fire, already less than it had been before, played off his face.

Eleni readied the flashlight on her phone and looked through the kitchen. She found an old butcher knife, dull to be sure. She remembered Ben using it to carve up an elk he'd killed, curing the meat on racks in the basement.

She thought briefly about giving the idea up altogether. They could huddle close together for warmth. Ben could be here any minute, likely with his gun, and he would know how to handle this better than she did. But then she thought of Jacob, and worse, thought of Jacob having some kind of attack, brought on by the freezing cold hurting his lungs. Ben might not show for hours, if he ever did. Chaz might wait a full day or two before coming back. The temperature was well below freezing, and it was pushing its way through the walls with every second that ticked by.

There was no choice to make, really. It was something that had to be done.

She pulled the heavy table she'd previously pushed in front of the door aside. The tiny, silver keys to the generators hung on a hook by the fridge. She grabbed them, hoping she'd remember how to reset what was likely a frozen battery, then fumbled at the small, sliding lock to open the basement door.

She wouldn't go to the one outside, only to the backup one in the basement.

The door swung open with a creak. She beamed her phone flashlight down the steps, the bluish light disappearing into the dark. At the base of the planks, the uneven dirt glistened with frost. Her breath whirled white in the dark, dissipating down into the black. She listened carefully and, hearing nothing but the wind, took her first step onto a creaking board.

It felt like being in a horror movie. Frozen cobwebs, leftover from the summertime, hung heavy from their posts like spun glass. The beam from her flashlight passed over one massive wasps' nest in the far corner, crystallized and sparkling like a heavy, horrid gem. The ancient laundry wringer still stood to one side, bulky and white, and across the small, dug-out space was the beige box that was the backup generator . . . right beside the two cellar doors which were, indeed, flung wide open, the slanting dirt floor going up and outside into utter darkness.

She stopped at the base of the steps and breathed deeply. Adjusting her grip on the knife and pointing it outward, she readied herself to jab anything that came near her. Her first thought was to creep up the dirt ramp and close the doors, but she remembered the wolf's breath against her leg and how if Chaz had hesitated a fraction of a second, it would have latched into her flesh. Her terror was complete. Instead, she crept to the generator and tried, as silently as possible, to open it.

She stuck one of the keys into the right-side lock. It wouldn't budge. She jerked it back and forth helplessly, feeling the panic in the pit of her stomach flicker and rise up like an out-of-control flame. Then she remembered. *Press down.* Pressing down on the lid, she turned the key. She felt it grudgingly push forward, then felt the lock release. Now, she had to do the same on the other side.

It was right as she was lifting the lid, listening to the creak of its hinges and the groan of the fiberglass, that she heard the squeaks.

Little, yipping squeaks, faint, from something small and inconsequential.

But then came the growl. The low, unwavering growl.

Eleni froze, hand still holding the lid up at an angle, key still in the lock. Her head stayed in place—she didn't dare turn it. She moved her eyes only, as far as she could, straining them. Dark, fuzzy shadows moved beneath the ancient laundry wringer. They were small, like puppies, wiggling in and out of a dug-out little hole that hadn't existed the last time she was here.

Then behind the small, tumbling puppy-shapes were the eyes. They caught the beam of her flashlight and shone, hovering above a snout full of bared teeth.

Eleni turned her head slowly before she moved her body, locking into full eye contact with the mother wolf.

It was a den.

Eleni stepped back, remembering the rules. She turned, angling her body back to the steps while maintaining total eye contact with the mother. Her flashlight washed over the den section of the basement. Four or five wolf pups milled around in a constant, rolling play. The mother stayed down on her haunches so she could peer at Eleni from beneath the legs of the laundry machine. When the light fully caught the mother's face, something inside of Eleni twisted and collapsed in on itself. It was like looking directly into the face of a nightmare, a death's head; the wolf's teeth were fully exposed, bared in a grotesque snarl, blood-red gums off-setting their brilliant, deadly white. Her eyes were clamped fully onto Eleni, whose feet, one after the other, were reaching back, step by step, over hard, uneven dirt, careful not to fall. Eleni was still clutching the knife in one hand, the phone in the other. The blade of the knife trembled, an extension of Eleni's own hand, pointing toward the mother.

Eleni hit the bottom step and almost fell back, realizing with both gratitude and nausea that she'd left the door to the kitchen open. It meant she could run back in, but it also meant she'd left Jacob fully exposed on the bed above.

It only took that half-stumble, her heel clopping up against the wooden plank and her balance wavering for a split second, for the mother wolf to be spurred to action. With a half-bark, half-growl, she was up, leaping out of her den and around the laundry machine, blocking the pups behind her with a protective stance.

Eleni steadied herself, re-established eye contact, and moved up another step. Then another. Almost there.

Growling low, the mother took a careful step closer.

And then Eleni turned and bolted, hearing the mother's growl crescendo into a barking declaration of the chase.

Eleni ran into the kitchen, stumbling over the linoleum with its air pockets, slamming the door shut, and sliding the lock back into place. As she did, there was a hard, heavy thud against the door, and the wood cracked in a long, thin line just left of center.

Tearing back into the living room, Eleni heard the scrabble of claws against the door and the cracking of the flimsy plywood boards. She yanked Jacob from the blankets and bundled him into her arms. His head lolled, his eyes snapped open, and he moaned at her, "Mommy, no." There was another sound of wood breaking—a longer, more definitive sound this time—a tearing apart of the boards.

Eleni ran to the ladder, pinning Jacob to her chest with her forearm, still holding the knife in one hand and her phone in the other. She clambered up, hugging each rung with her wrists. When she slipped, she dropped the knife, and it clattered to the floor below. She could hear the breath of the wolf, no longer slamming into the door but straining as she pushed her way through whatever opening she had made. Eleni kept going higher, leaving the knife farther behind with each step. She screamed, "Jacob, hold on! Hold on to Mommy!" and in a half-asleep, half-fussy way, he threw his arms around her neck, letting her use both hands to climb. She reached the loft, hoisted him over the top rung of the ladder, and threw herself after him right as she heard the wolf's claws scrabble into the living room, over the wooden floor.

Eleni pushed Jacob back, who was full into tears once again, turned, and lifted her booted foot to kick as hard as she could against the ladder. It was sloped, not perfectly vertical, and the footholds were wide, so it was conceivable the wolf could climb up. She kicked against the top rung and the sides until she heard and felt the wood splitting. On one side, the bolt securing the ladder in place pulled from the wall in a cloud of plaster dust. With one final kick, the ladder was disconnected, falling into the living room. She heard a yelp from the wolf as it cracked over the animal's back, then the ladder crashed onto the floor, breaking.

7

THE ATTACK

Eleni breathed as hard and as painfully as she ever had in her life. Her heart pummeled the inside of her ribcage, everything in agony. She'd acted on pure instinct and couldn't even recall the run from the basement steps to the loft. She only remembered the panicked blur of it, the unhooking of mind from reasoned thought so she could descend into rapid action.

She crept to the edge of the loft floor, which had no guard-rail. One fractured wooden spike, part of the ladder, remained sticking up, still bolted. Lying entirely on her stomach, she peered down into the living room below. Light from the fire was dim; just a few faint, orange shadows tinged the room. The ladder laid across the floor, one side roughly split in a long, diagonal gash midway up the rungs. Right beside the ladder was the wolf, who limped slightly, then sat and stared.

Her fangs were no longer bared. She was simply looking up, trying to figure out her next move. Her eyes locked onto Eleni's, and they shone with intelligence. They didn't seem filled with malice so much as uncomplicated forward momentum. Eleni came too close to her pups, and this was how it was going to be. The mother wolf was beautiful with her white belly and peppering of dark fur down the back of her head and spine. She was larger, too, than Eleni would have expected.

Eleni eased back out of sight, seeing the wolf take a step closer to the loft as she did. She heard the touch of claws against plaster as the wolf went up on her hind legs, front paws pressed to the wall, to sniff after her. Then the claws clacked back down onto the floor.

Jacob was lying on his side in a rag-like heap, sobbing. Eleni patted him, then rubbed his back harder, then fully curled around him, pulling him into her, like two puppies snuggled together. He hitched and shook, and she realized just how badly she herself still trembled. Her hands were numb, and she realized she might be going into shock, so she started to consciously talk herself out of it.

"It's ok, it's ok, it's ok," she said, over and over, gripping Jacob. He breathed a deep, ragged breath. "It's ok. Just stay back here. We'll stay back, far from the edge. Understand? No going near the edge."

If you fall, there will be no more Jacob.

Arching her neck back, head still on the floor, she looked around the loft. Her phone was still in sight, thank God; it had fallen onto the loft floor when they'd scrambled off the ladder, and the beam from the flashlight now illuminated the small space. It was easily twice as dusty up here as it had been down below. Large boxes were stacked up against the back wall under a sheet, and one twin mattress was pushed to the right side, up against the stone chimney. Maybe some warmth would leak through those stones.

She pushed with her booted feet against the floor, dragging Jacob along with her, moving them both back as far as they could go until they came up against the boxes.

"I'm sorry, sweetheart, I'm sorry," she said, kissing and smoothing his hair. "It's ok now, it's ok, it's ok."

He inhaled in a painful rasp, his entire body tensing against hers, and that's when Eleni realized . . .

She silently cursed herself for not realizing it the moment they'd gone up in the loft.

He was having an attack.

She jerked upright, now sitting beside him as he lay prone on the loft floor in his flannel moose outfit. He looked at her with desperate, scared eyes, mouth opening as wide as it could go, as if that would help make his throat open, as well.

"Oh, God, oh no, oh sweetie . . ."

He flailed his arms at her, eyes bugging slightly.

"Ok, ok." She tried to smooth out his posture, lay him down flat. "Breathe, it's ok, calm, in, out."

Flat on his back, his body continued to twitch. He continued to look at her, pleading, ragged breaths like nails on a chalkboard, each one making her cringe.

She went back to the edge of the loft to look down.

The mother wolf, sitting now, jumped back up on all fours when she saw Eleni and moved slightly closer to the wall. Eleni drew back. She put a hand on Jacob's chest, trying to feel the motion of his breathing inside him.

The medicine bag sat on the dining table, its detachable black strap dangling over the edge toward the floor. It was less than ten feet away from where the wolf stood, gazing up after them.

"Easy, easy," she repeated as she ran gentle hands over Jacob, her mind racing and desperate. Her eyes darted around the loft, searching for something, anything that might help.

She clambered to her feet, legs like jelly, and tossed the sheet off the boxes to rip open the cardboard top of the one closest to her. Lots of papers. Lots of nothing, really—she brought the nothing out by the handful, letting it scatter on the floor. Toward the bottom were some heavy, ancient books.

She pulled them up from beneath the weight of the remaining papers, piling them in her arms. Wilderness survival guides, military tactics, guerrilla fighting—there was a definite theme to the reading material. Many of them were hardcover with broken spines, obviously well-read. Bending slightly so as not to hit her head on the ceiling, she went back to the edge, feeling a wave of vertigo. The wolf observed her, head cocked to one side.

"Get out of here!" Eleni shrieked, not even recognizing her own hysterical voice. She pulled the first book from the stack in her left arm and hurled it down. The pages fanned out in mid-air, making it spiral. It landed right in front of the wolf's paws, making her take two steps back.

"Out!" Eleni screamed even louder, more hysterical than before. Back home, multiple neighbors would have heard her in their adjoining apartments. Here, though her voice filled the space, it would vanish right beyond the walls. She threw another book, and the wolf skirted it, then paced around it in a semi-circle. The animal stretched her head toward the book, sniffing the musty pages.

"OUT!" Eleni lifted one of the heavier tomes, a hard-back, thousand-page doorstop, and reared it up behind her, throwing it with all her force. It tumbled through the air, then came down smack on the wolf's back between her shoulder blades, approximately where the falling ladder had already hit.

The wolf let out a yelp and skittered over to the side, low to the ground and with legs slightly splayed. She circled the dining room table, her fur brushing against the strap to the medicine bag where it hung. She eyed Eleni with hostility and annoyance, then skulked into the kitchen.

"Oh, yes, yes," Eleni breathed, putting down the few extra books. She looked directly down, judging the drop into the living room. She eyed the ladder, laying across the living room floor, unsure whether it would be able to support any kind of weight if she propped it back up, with the one side broken.

"Ok." She went and got the sheet that had been on the boxes and began, fast, to twist it up into a rope. About every three feet or so along its length, she tied a knot.

Jacob watched her from his place on the floor, moving only his eyes, the rest of him still but struggling.

"Mommy's going to get your medicine," she whispered. "I promise. It's going to be ok. Calm. Be calm, sweetheart."

He watched her, trapped.

She went back to the edge. The wolf wasn't in sight. She heard rustling coming from the kitchen and wondered if the creature was getting into the cabinets and the food. That would be fine with her. She looked straight down and saw the dull butcher knife where it lay, the metal catching a faint gleam from the dying fire. Ok.

The nub of ladder-post that remained attached to the side of the drop was the only place to secure her sheet-rope. She looped it around the post and tied it as best she could, Jacob's breath a staccato beat in the background.

If it wasn't secure, she didn't know how to make it any better. There was no time to pick up a survival guide and figure out how to build a stronger ladder. If she didn't act fast, Jacob was going to go into anaphylactic shock.

She listened carefully. Stillness. She caught the whisper of an animal's snorts as it prodded its way into a bag of food somewhere out of sight.

There was no choice.

Gripping the sheet, she swung her legs over the ledge.

"I love you. I love you, baby."

She pushed herself off.

8

SURVIVAL

When Eleni first swung off the ledge, turning to brace her legs against the wall, they made a banging sound, and she froze, holding herself out like a mountain climber, to see if the wolf would come running back. She didn't.

Awkwardly, Eleni walked her way down the wall, gripping the sheet, fists above the knots. She watched, with each maneuver down, as Jacob slowly rose up and out of her sight. She was now right above the living room floor, and she carefully picked one foot off the wall and lowered it down.

As soon as her feet were on the floor, she let go of the sheet, arms shaking, dipped, and picked up the butcher knife from where it had fallen, listening intently.

Running parallel to the sound of Jacob's labored breathing up in the loft, there were sounds of claws clacking on the kitchen floor, and a sound she remembered from having a dog in her childhood, of the animal circling once or twice and then laying down. It sounded like the wolf had gone near the basement door, closer to her pups.

Eleni took a careful step forward, praying the floors wouldn't squeak beneath her weight. She half-slid, half-walked, keeping her head turned toward the opening into the kitchen, her eyes darting back and forth from there to the medicine bag. The distance between her and her goal was so short, but she knew if she rushed it, it would all be over.

She pushed her foot forward, and the floor let out a low groan beneath her, the floorboard springy under her step. Freezing again, she waited. Looking at the opening into the dark kitchen, she could imagine, so perfectly, the wolf coming toward her out of the shadows, now on a level playing field, those teeth against their blood-red gums bared once more. She waited, heard the inhale-exhale of a creature that was settled down, then continued.

She was there. She was right beside the table.

Without moving her feet again, she leaned over and lifted the strap of the medicine bag. Silently, it rose up off the table, and she slung the strap over her head and across her chest, pushing the bulk of the bag behind her. She had it. It was hers. *I'm coming, Jacob.*

She looked over, trying to assess how to get back in the loft. Eleni didn't feel at all certain the ladder would support any weight; the one side of it was completely broken, and half of the rungs, only firmly secure on one side, would likely give way beneath her. She thought, then grabbed the back of a wooden chair from the dining table, lifted it carefully, and brought it with her.

She shuffled back the way she'd come, trying to skirt around the spot where she knew the floor would squeak, although she didn't entirely avoid making noise. The added weight of the chair didn't help. Still, though, the wolf didn't appear.

I'm coming, I'm coming, she thought, listening for Jacob. His breathing pattern had changed into a slower and deeper *ah-ohhh, ah-ohhh* beat, worse than before. A sharp breath in, then a much larger breath whooshing out. She was almost there.

At the base of her sheet-rope, she put the chair down, then stooped to grab the heavy books and pile them on the chair for more height. She kept the entryway to the kitchen in the corner of her eye. The knife was still in her hand, the blade scraping faintly against the chair as she positioned it.

She lifted one heavy, booted foot onto the seat of the chair, then pulled the other up after it to position it on the unstable books. Slipping the knife into the front pocket of the medicine bag, she gripped the twisted sheet with both hands.

If she hadn't been standing on the books, if she hadn't yet gone up on the chair, she would have been fine.

She cast one more glance toward the kitchen entryway, and at that exact moment, something fuzzy and determined ran out of the darkness and in her direction. It was the anticipation that did it, waiting for the wolf, expecting the wolf . . . but this was no wolf. It was a rat, smaller even than a wolf pup, just hugging the periphery of the room and making its way from point A to B. But the expectation, the fear—they caused her to jump and twist where she stood, the glossy cover of the top book slipping and sliding beneath her. The book shot out from under her, and her foot came down at an awkward angle. She felt herself falling backward like a bad sight gag; the entire world swirled and swiveled and became something unintelligible. She came down on her back, flat on the floor, head missing the brick fireplace by mere inches. The chair toppled over with a noisy crash, and she grunted in spite of herself.

Adrenaline did its job. She sprang back up to her feet, fumbling for the knife. In her panic, she couldn't manage to get the medicine bag pulled to her front; it remained stubbornly twisted behind her back.

The wolf moved faster than Eleni's adrenaline. Her canine body, curled in the kitchen, leapt into action, trotting quickly into the room, fangs out. Eleni moved back, banging against the fireplace. She couldn't get to the knife, didn't even know if she still had the knife or if it had fallen out somewhere. The wolf charged, and Eleni lunged out of the way, dodging her, like playing tag with Jacob in the park. The animal spun, sleek and smooth, gliding toward her prey in the way she was built for. She was designed to be a predator, and Eleni fell beside the fireplace, lifting an arm to block the animal's attack. She was knocked onto her back, the weight of the animal crushing her down.

With every ounce of her strength, Eleni held the mother wolf back, fangs mere inches from her face. The teeth snapped, and slobber broke away from the mouth in free-flying drops. Eleni curled her legs up beneath the wolf and kicked out, launching the animal back.

Just a few inches to breathe.

They always see their "in."

Eleni saw her "in."

She reached out and grabbed the small hand axe from behind the woodpile. The wolf lunged again, but this time, Eleni swung the axe in an arc toward it, catching the wolf in the throat.

The wolf let out an almost-human cry of pain and skittered away from Eleni. The axe fell between them, the blade now glazed with blood. Eleni retrieved it and brandished it toward the animal as she got back on her feet.

Blood dripped from the wolf's throat. Despite the injury, she moved toward Eleni again, and Eleni swiped at her with the axe. She backed up.

The wolf took stuttering steps away, across the room, maintaining eye contact. She knew, without having to be taught, never to look away from a predator. She left an abstract jumble of crimson spots in the center of the room before retreating to the far corner. Eyes still glaring, she crawled under the tablecloth on the side-table, disappearing from view.

9

THE CLIMB

Eleni stood for a long moment, her own breathing so loud in her ears that it took a few long beats before it started to meld with the sound of Jacob's breathing. She suddenly heard his breath, still ragged and strained, as something apart from hers, as if fear itself had made all the sounds of the world blend together in a fever dream, and now they were separating themselves back out.

She fumbled where she stood, taking a half-step back to look up to the loft, then back to the end table with its dusty, low-hanging tablecloth. The cloth was draped at a diagonal, with one end slightly up. She squinted, trying to see the wolf beneath. The trail of blood drops ended by the dining table, no trace of them disappearing down the center of the slightly raised opening. She couldn't hear the animal. No breath from inside that small sanctuary stirred the sheet. Was she dead? Was she dying?

Eleni moved for the loft again, wanting to return to Jacob as quickly as possible, but stopped. The door to the basement was destroyed, and if this wolf had gotten in, there was no telling what else might follow. She couldn't go back up, leaving it like this. Carefully, back hugging the wall, she went to the kitchen.

Sure enough, some of the bags of food had been torn open. Animal crackers littered the floor in front of the fridge.

She quickly turned, making sure the wolf wasn't following her.

Nothing there.

The door to the basement had split almost entirely down the middle. Cold air gushed through the opening, easily wide enough for another animal to come through. With the smell of blood and food, it wouldn't take long for something else to make its way there.

She tried to press the broken wood back together. It would slide into place, under her guiding hands, then ease back apart when she stepped away. She arranged it as best she could, trying to move fast, then turned to the large, wooden table she'd pushed aside when she went downstairs to inspect the generator.

She got behind it, placing the axe on top to keep the weapon within reach. The blood on its handle smudged onto the tabletop in an arc. She pushed the table, having to not care about the screeching noise it made.

With the table pressed against the door, it was held mostly closed, helping the heat stay in and anything else with teeth stay out. There was still a splintered gap near the bottom, possibly large enough for a pup to squeeze through, but it was the best she could do.

She took the axe up again and hurried back to the living room. The wolf was still out of sight. Eleni lifted the broken ladder, flipping it so the half with the rungs still secured on either side was now on top. She righted the chair, climbed up, then transferred her weight over to the ladder, which cracked and swayed. Freezing, she steadied herself; it would break entirely any second. She hurried up one rung, two—finally scrambling up and over and back onto the floor of the loft, breathing hard.

The wolf was still nowhere to be seen.

Jacob had moved from his position, now curled further back toward the boxes in a pathetic heap. She hurried to him.

"It's ok, baby. Mommy's here. I'm here. We're safe."

What a liar you are.

She fumbled the medicine bag off of her shoulder, tearing open the zipper. A plastic baggie filled with Elmo bandages and a tube of disinfecting ointment fell out. She pulled out each component of the battery-operated nebulizer—he was too small to be able to use an inhaler properly—and began putting together the tubing, mask, and mouthpiece.

He looked up at her, and she saw the trails of tears that had trekked from the corners of his eyes.

"It's ok, it's ok," she said, getting the mask over his face and helping him sit up, his back propped against her. She poured the medicine into the cup on the machine and turned it on.

She worried, for a split second, that at some point during the journey, due to the cold or being jostled around, that the nebulizer had broken. But then it came to life, its mechanical whir filling the loft. The mist poured out from the machine, carrying the medicine, filling the mask that covered his mouth and nose. She rubbed his chest.

"Breathe deep. Breathe deep for Mommy."

He tried, but he couldn't. The breaths were shallow and painful, the medicine only going so far.

Eleni dropped her head, praying, *Please, please*, her comforting hand not budging from his chest.

The first time Jacob had a severe attack, he'd been playing on the floor of their apartment on a second-hand area rug. His colorful blocks were spread around him like chunky confetti. Eleni had been sitting on the couch, looking through her bills for the month—and all of a sudden, he started wheezing.

First, she'd thought it was just part of his play and that he was experimenting with making different sounds. But then he'd dropped the block he was holding and looked at her, and she saw how his brow furrowed and how his color changed. Asthma hadn't even occurred to her; at first, she'd thought he must have swallowed something he picked up off the floor. Cursing herself for not cleaning more carefully, she wondered what he could have gotten. She even forced his head back to look down his throat despite how his ragged breaths intensified at the motion. Finally, not two minutes later, she'd picked him up and ran for her used car to speed toward the emergency room.

It took ten minutes to get there. At every stoplight, every stop sign, she hated the world, thinking to herself, *He's dying, he's dying right now, and I don't know what to do.* Finally, she'd pulled up in front of the ER, leaving the car with its blinkers on in the ambulance lane, and ran inside with him, crying out, "He can't breathe! He can't breathe!"

She'd bulled past two people waiting in line to check in, who gave her dirty looks that softened when they saw the baby in her arms, his lips tinted blue, his hands gripping her hair as if she could save him from drowning. The nurses immediately took him back. Eleni's car was towed, and she was fined, but she didn't care. She got off the hook at traffic court when she told the story.

She had never been so relieved in all her life as when she watched Jacob lie on that hospital bed, his small body fitting mostly on the pillow, a nebulizer mask strapped over his face. The desperate fight for his breath had subsided, and his body slowly began to relax and breathe normally, all the tension draining out of it. He'd looked up at her, that little face almost entirely under clear plastic but for his eyes and forehead, and the look in his eyes had calmed. She'd stroked his head and kept saying, "I love you, I love you," over and over because there was nothing else to say.

He had severe asthma, and their lives were never going to be quite the same. Eleni would never go anywhere again without the nebulizer strapped to her body. She would never truly get lost in her own thoughts again; part of her would always be alert, listening for changes in Jacob's breathing, even the slightest whisper of a problem. Everything she could sell that was worth much of anything, she sold to help afford what she needed for his care—all the things her pathetic insurance plan didn't cover.

Just remembering Jacob on that hospital bed was enough to bring tears to her eyes, even on a good day. Tonight, the memory was enough to make her borderline hysterical. She kept telling him to breathe in, then would count "1-2-3," trying to make him hold in the air with the medicine as best he could so it could settle in his lungs.

He wasn't able to hold it in; he was barely able to breathe it in at all. But after several agonizing minutes, the same relaxation suddenly broke through the tension in his body, as it had on that night of the first attack. The stiffness ran out of him like it had gone down a drain. All the muscles and rigid limbs suddenly went loose. He eased more comfortably back into her, folding down slightly, exhausted from the ordeal. His breath moved in and out, and while there was a slight rasp to it, it was no longer a struggle. The inflammation in his airways was going down. His throat would be sore, but he was able to breathe again.

"That's it. That's it, sweetie," Eleni said, kissing his hair, relieved in the same way she'd been at the hospital. Her face tilted upward, eyes squeezed shut, tears tracking down her cheeks, in a completely wordless gesture of thanks. She held Jacob close to her.

His nebulizer made a sputtering noise, signaling that the medicine cup was now almost empty. Eleni let it run out entirely, then switched it off.

"Good job, good job, Jacob," she said, soothing, as she took the mask off his face. He smacked his lips a little, dazed, touching the mask as she pulled it away. "Very good boy."

"Hurts, Mommy."

"I know it does, sweetie. But you were very, very brave. It's all over now."

"I don't want that—never again."

"I know, sweetie. I hope you never have it again."

"Never again."

"I know." She took a deep breath, trying to follow her own advice about holding it in, 1-2-3, allowing it to help calm her nervous system. "Sometimes, these tough things happen. But we gotta be brave and stay calm and just breathe deep, right?"

"Yeah."

"And it passed."

Jacob nodded, trying to follow the logic.

"Here. Get cozy."

She laid him down on the twin mattress, covering him with the blanket; she rubbed the dust on it downward, toward where he positioned his feet, away from his face. It rolled up in tight, horizontal bunches under her swiping palm.

"Wait," she said, lifting him to sit up again. She pulled off her scarf and spread it over the age-worn, compressed pillow. The pillow had been covered by the blanket, so it wasn't that dusty, but just in case . . . her scarf would give him a little bit of a barrier.

She laid his head down and stroked his cheek.

"Sing, Mommy," he commanded, wiped out by the entire experience. "Sing 'Sunshine.'"

Eleni often sang "You Are My Sunshine," only she changed the words. She didn't like that "Sunshine" went away. She remembered being a child herself and loving the tune until one day, she asked her mother to clarify what it meant. When she knew that Sunshine had gone, she'd cried and cried, inconsolable. Her mother never sang it to her again after that.

Eleni sang it, though. She just recreated it as she went, turning the sad parts into joyful parts. "When I awoke, dear, I was mistaken, so I hung my head, and I cried," Eleni would turn into "when I awoke, dear, oh there you were, dear . . .

and, so happy, I sighed." Her lyrics were awkward, choppy, forced to fit into the beat sometimes, but Jacob loved them. He fell asleep to this song more often than not.

"You are my sunshine, my only sunshine."

She reached across Jacob, feeling the rocks of the chimney to see if they held any warmth from the fire. They were chilly. The light from the fire was almost entirely out now, although the flashlight from her phone, lying across the floor on the other side of the loft, still beamed up at the ceiling, covering them in a bluish glow.

"You make me happy when skies are gray."

She took off her parka and draped it over Jacob for extra warmth.

"You'll never know, dear, how much I love you."

It was going to get very, very cold.

"Please don't take my sunshine away."

10

THE BRAWL

She half-dozed with Jacob, the two of them keeping each other warm until the full reality of where they were and all they had gone through came back to her. Then her eyes opened wide and sleep felt like a foreign concept.

Her phone read 2:03 a.m. She crawled off the mattress and looked down toward the front door as if just by looking at it, she could will Ben to appear, back with them at last. What would he think when he first came in to see the broken ladder and the drops of blood? The small axe, the blood on its edge now congealed, rested on the loft floor near where she had climbed back up.

What if she heard Ben being attacked outside by wolves when he arrived? What would she do?

She took her deep breaths—1, 2, 3—and told herself he'd have a gun, that he'd lived here most of his life, and he'd know exactly what to do. He wouldn't need her help. She crept closer to the drop into the living room and searched for the wolf. Nothing. The tablecloth didn't stir. She wondered if the creature was lying in that pseudo-cave, dead. She wondered how long before dead things started to smell.

The charge on her phone was getting low because of the flashlight. Around thirty percent. She should probably turn it off, but the fire was almost completely out now, just glowing embers they couldn't see from where they were, and she couldn't bear the thought of being in the dark, knowing there were monsters so close to them.

She turned to the boxes.

It was entirely possible Ben had some matches or candles or even lanterns up here, storing away all the things one could need out in the wilderness. It was also possible, maybe . . .

That there was a gun.

She crawled on hands and knees to the back wall, kneeling to open and rifle through boxes. They mostly held papers and old photographs.

A rusting flask was at the bottom of the first box; she had picked it up at some tourist trap and given it to him on his birthday when they'd spent the weekend in Juneau. Rolling his eyes, he'd said that someone who lived in Alaska didn't need a flask that said "Alaska" to impress all his friends. He'd kissed her anyway, though, looping an arm around her neck to pull her close and plant one on her forehead.

A pile of glossy photographs gleamed up at her from the bottom of a box, and she pulled them out. They were of them: at a bonfire, before quitting their jobs, then on the train. There was one of her zip-lining, screaming and kicking her feet up above the thick Tongass National Forest. Then she found one of them lying in bed, lazy and happy, kissing, a co-selfie.

She'd printed these to put up on the refrigerator. It occurred to her now that she'd left them up after she and Ben were gone, as a testament to what had been in the cabin. It felt important that the love and the joy that had once filled its walls be somehow commemorated, even as it stood empty. Perhaps she'd also hoped that if he ever came back, even secretly, he'd see them and think of her.

Then she remembered: the cops had been here. The cops had been through everything, including those pictures, taking them down and checking the back of each one, searching for captions that could become clues. All these boxes, all of Ben's belongings, would have been explored. They hadn't bothered to put things back where they'd been; everything was thrown into these boxes after it had been pored over, then shoved up here. All they cared about was connecting Ben with Aimee.

But there was no connection with Aimee.

She kept the pictures out and lined them up against the wall across from the mattress. Something to show Jacob when he woke in the morning.

That's me and your daddy. That's him.

Once, while leaving the playground, Jacob had said to her, "I don't have a daddy." She'd been taken aback by the statement. It wasn't said with any degree of self-pity or sadness; it was just stated as a fact. Not for the first time, she marveled at the realization that this little person, this little live baby doll, was formulating thoughts and theories about his life and starting to put them in words.

"You have a daddy," she said, then wondered if she should have said it. It was likely only going to confuse him more. "Your daddy loves you a lot. He just had to go away."

"Why away?"

"For work."

It was the quickest, easiest answer to come to mind.

Eleni opened another box, then gasped quietly. A lantern!

She tore it from its packaging, fumbling to pop open the battery compartment. Empty, of course. But double A's . . . she reached for the medicine bag, which contained a twenty-pack of backup double A's for Jacob's nebulizer. She said a silent prayer of thanks that she'd gotten the kind of nebulizer that took regular batteries, then fumbled out four of them, slicing her finger on the plastic casing.

It worked. As the light flooded the space, she felt like she had her first true exhale of the night. She set the lantern in the center of the floor and turned off the flashlight on her phone to conserve the battery, tucking it into the front pocket of her sweatshirt.

Jacob did a deep inhale-exhale, sound asleep. Eleni, basking in the glow of the lantern, sat against the far wall and looked at him, then looked around the loft. She sucked on the cut finger before rubbing some ointment into it and putting on an Elmo bandage.

She'd only spent the night up there on one other occasion.

Ben kept the extra mattress in case friends stopped by. On a few occasions, Chaz slept up in the loft while Ben and Eleni slept down below. He'd come over, do some heavy drinking, play some cards, and manage to get up the ladder without breaking his neck before passing out. Eleni could remember looking up at least once in the middle of the night to see him peering down at them voyeuristically.

That other friend had stayed there, too . . . what was his name? Mark. Mark, with the hooded eyes and set jaw, whose personality seemed to hover between boy-next-door friendly and edgy recluse, as if he couldn't make up his mind. He was a childhood friend of Ben's. They'd grown up together in Alaska, and Mark had even followed Ben to Oregon a few months after he left when Ben got Mark a job. They'd both wound up back in Alaska a short while later. Ben and Eleni had hung out with him in one of the dive bars in town a few times, spots where Jack London had thrown back drinks. A few times, Mark had spent the night in the cabin so that he and Ben could get up early in the morning to go hunting when the animals were most likely to be out, serene and undisturbed.

But Eleni had only stayed up here once, Ben apologetic and pacing down below. When she slid under the blanket with Jacob earlier, the feel of it took her back to that night, only for a split second, the way sensory memories could. Back came the sensation of being curled up, her pre-baby body tighter, pulling the blanket up around her ears, wondering what she should do and if she should do anything at all.

Ben had screwed up, and they both knew it. She also knew, deep down, that over the course of the night, of turning it over in her mind and sleeping fitfully, that she'd second guess herself, wonder if it was really a big deal, wonder if she shouldn't even be a little bit flattered. But at first, in those darkened moments, listening to Ben whisper, "*Shit,*" down below, there had been a part of her that was fully aware, a part saying that the next time she managed to get into town, she shouldn't come back here.

"He assaulted some girl in Anchorage, you know!" Ben had cried out, as if this revelation would make the entire night ok. She didn't reply.

She knew once she replied, once he engaged her in a dialogue, it was done. He'd suck her back in; he'd seem reasonable, sweet even, like someone who'd just made a mistake but had been led there by genuinely rational thinking.

Eleni wasn't ready for it to be done. She kept picturing Paul, lying in the middle of the street, the back of his head cracked open against the concrete. There were no hospitals in town, only a small clinic with a nurse practitioner. Someone called the NP, and people with first-aid training flocked around, checking Paul's pulse.

An hour earlier, they'd all been sitting together having a beer.

Paul was one of the guys they'd worked with on the train. Now that they'd quit, most of their former co-workers had simply slipped out of their lives without comment, but Paul stayed in friendly touch, meeting up with them on occasion and updating them on what everyone back at work was doing. They heard who was hooking up, then breaking up, and heard the sordid tale of someone the managers fired when they learned he was keeping pots he'd stolen from the kitchen full of piss in his cabin (instead of going to the restroom). Ben liked Paul, generally speaking, and liked how Paul seemed to view him and Eleni as a unit, mainly addressing Ben when they talked. Eleni only listened, bolstering their conversations with her enthusiastic silence.

Then Paul made a mistake.

He was talking about some girl he'd slept with from town but who he'd seen with a different guy the next night. The conversation had been flowing along, fast, bawdy, beer after beer consumed. It was the kind of conversation where people were having such a good time that things slipped out.

"No loyalty, you know?" Paul joked, then he reached out and put a hand over Eleni's on the table. "I should've grabbed you when I had the chance, before this guy got his hooks in you."

He chuckled, and after an almost imperceptible pause, Ben had chuckled, but Eleni could tell it wasn't his regular laugh.

"You hitting on my girlfriend, P?" Ben asked, glaring at Paul as he sipped his beer.

"Mourning what could have been!" Paul said, still making light of it. "What do you say, Ells, come back with me to my cabin tonight, forget this asshole?"

Eleni smiled, nervous, but withdrew her hand.

"Should've followed my instincts," Ben was saying, staring down at the table, then lifting his eyes to Paul's. "Knew not to trust you."

"Sorry, sucker!" Paul said, still joking, then he caught on to the edge in Ben's voice, and his eyes began to dart back and forth between Ben and Eleni.

"Oh, c'mon," he said. "I'm just kidding."

"That's what you kid about? Fucking my girlfriend?"

"Hey, c'mon man—"

"You want to fuck my girlfriend?"

Ben stood at that point, glaring down at Paul, who was looking up at him, wide-mouthed, seemingly baffled by the turn things had taken.

"No . . . I only meant, you know . . . Eleni's a great girl. I want a girlfriend like that."

"So, you want *my* girlfriend?"

Paul exhaled, shaking his head, looking away. "That's not what I meant, man."

"If it's not what you meant, then why have you said it three fucking times already?"

Ben leaned over the table, face close to Paul's, forcing Paul to back up.

"Get out of my *face*, asshole," Paul barked, now standing too, and that word, *asshole*, spoken as some sort of razzing joke moments earlier, now took on a sharper verve, a challenge. Paul took a step toward Ben, trying to drive him back in the other direction.

Eleni stood because they were both standing. She put a hand on Ben.

"It's fine, really, it's fine," she said, but she knew the issue here wasn't actually whether or not *she* was fine. It wasn't that he was concerned her honor had been affronted or that she felt threatened. It was that *he* felt threatened.

"Don't tell me what to do," he said, pushing Paul back. Paul, for a moment, seemed like he was going to take a swing. The entire bar paused, watching them, waiting to see what would happen. A waitress ran to get a manager.

Then Paul's eyes landed on Eleni, and his face softened. He took a step back. He didn't want to fight out of some kind of respect for her.

"You know, Ben, everyone back at work says you're a psycho, and they're right," Paul said, grabbing his jacket off the back of his chair. Then, to her, "Sorry, Eleni, but when you come to your senses and want to leave this fucker, give me a call."

It wasn't said as a come-on. At least, that wasn't how Eleni heard it. She heard it as an offer of help.

Ben heard it differently. Or maybe he didn't. But either way—whether Paul was offering Eleni romance or help—he didn't like it.

As Paul went for the door, Ben followed, hot on his heels. The moment they were outside, Ben shoved him, hard, off the wooden plank porch. The mountains loomed over the old-timey, saloon-like buildings lining the street. Paul stumbled, turned, and took a swing at Ben, right as Eleni got outside. Ben partially dodged it, the punch landing on his upraised arm, then swung his fist so hard into Paul's face that Paul fell back in the street, cracking his skull against the macadam, out cold.

Later, when the cops came, the only two cops in town, people told them it had been two guys fighting, not that Ben had attacked Paul. Ben told the cops Paul had harassed his girlfriend. They'd turned to Eleni to confirm this, but Eleni was in tears, and Ben told them she was still shaken up. When they told her she'd need to come to the station the next day to give a statement, she nodded.

Paul was taken to the airstrip on the edge of town. A helicopter came to air-lift him to the hospital in Juneau. Ben had permission to leave the "scene" with Eleni, and they drove back to the cabin silently. He waited until the truck pulled up in front of the porch, two miles from town with only a faint bluish light in the sky from the midnight sun, to begin speaking.

"He was wrong to say what he said," he kept insisting as Eleni stayed quiet beside him. He said different variations of that, over and over again, until she finally just unbuckled her seatbelt and nodded toward the cabin, wanting to be done with the onslaught of his words.

As they walked toward the door, he made his final push. "So, you'll tell them, right? How he was harassing you, saying that stuff? How he grabbed you?"

"He didn't grab me."

"Have you lost your mind?" Ben said as he opened the door, his face now inches from hers. She scurried inside, trying to put some distance between them. "He completely grabbed your hand even after you told him to knock it off."

She looked at him, brow furrowed.

"I didn't . . . it wasn't . . ."

"Ells," he said, looking deep into her eyes as if she were having a mental breakdown. "You told him he was making you uncomfortable, and then he grabbed your hand and tried to pull you closer."

Eleni backed away in earnest.

"Just—"

"Where are you going?"

"I'm going to sleep up there tonight."

"Hell you are. Let's talk about this."

"I want some space. Just give me some space to think about it."

"There's nothing to think about!"

"It's been a crazy night. I just want some space."

"It's been crazy because he scared you. That's why you're not thinking straight. I had to look out for you."

"Let's just get some sleep and figure it out in the morning."

She'd finally managed to get past him and climb into the loft, making him promise to give her space and stay in the living room, but he didn't let up. He continued to pace and make his claims down below. Throughout the night, she heard over and over how Paul had actually once assaulted a girl at a bar in Anchorage, landing her in the hospital. Then about how Paul had been touching Eleni's leg under the table, which Eleni said didn't happen. Ben kept saying over and over that it had, reminding her that she'd "pulled back, played it off like it was an accident, probably hadn't thought about it again after that," but that it had, in fact, happened.

At some point, Ben, feigning broken-heartedness, lay across the bed in the living area, trying to keep his closing eyes fixed on the loft. It wasn't like she could have left, though.

The next morning, Eleni woke up but only continued to stare at the ceiling until she heard the creak of the ladder. Ben climbed carefully into the loft, eying her with deference. "Is it ok that I come up?" he asked after he was already there, kneeling beside her bed.

She gazed up at him with sore, red eyes.

"I just love you so fucking much, sweetie," he said, exhaling on the *so fucking much*, like the weight of all the love was making him deflate. "I'm trying to look out for you. You're so innocent. You're not even from around here. You don't know what these guys can be like. You have to trust me. Don't you trust me to know what's really going on?"

She looked at him and gave a half-shrug.

"I know what's really going on. I wouldn't have done it if I didn't. You're my top priority. You."

But she knew it hadn't really been about her.

"You gotta let the cops know I was just taking care of you."

This went on for a while. At some point, she said, "I could maybe tell them I think it was a misunderstanding."

He shook his head, emphatic. "There was no misunderstanding, Eleni. He was trying to force himself on you."

Somehow, throughout the course of the preceding twelve hours, the narrative had gone from Paul making inappropriate comments to Paul roughly grabbing her hand to Paul touching her leg secretively under the table to Paul now, somehow, trying to force himself on her. "He wasn't," she kept saying, and Ben kept saying that she hadn't noticed, or just thought it was by accident, or wasn't remembering it right, or had been drunk. At some point, she began really trying to pull up in her memory things she was pretty sure hadn't happened.

Around 11 a.m., Ben grew desperate.

"If we don't get down there now, they're going to come for me," he said.

Aren't we a team?

84

They drove to the small, two-room police station on the edge of town. A back room contained two holding cells, and the front room had a desk and a couple of chairs. Eleni and Ben sat across from Officer Kent, an older man. Another officer, Pete Logan, about their same age, puttered around in the background before excusing himself so the statement-giving felt more confidential. Logan nodded at Eleni as if he was tipping his hat, old-fashioned, respectful, then was gone. Ben pulled his chair close to the desk and leaned forward, so he loomed much larger in Kent's vision than Eleni did. Then he reached one hand behind him, keeping it firmly over Eleni's hands in her lap.

"So, good news is, there's no permanent damage," Kent told them. "You accidentally kill some guy, no matter what he was doing to your girl, this is a whole different kind of conversation."

Kent eyed Eleni. "So, what did happen?"

Eleni shrugged, got teary. "Sorry," she choked after an unreasonably long pause. "I'm just still kind of upset."

"Take your time. It's understandable. You want water?"

She shook her head no, then spoke.

"I just . . . I guess maybe Paul liked me, and things got a little inappropriate."

"Inappropriate how?"

She looked at Ben. His head had swiveled toward her, eyes like a hawk.

"Just . . . some kind of tasteless jokes . . . about sleeping with me . . . and, um . . . I don't know, tried to hold my hand."

"And he was trying to touch her legs under the table," Ben put in. "Eleni was trying to play it off because it was weird, you know, but he kept doing it."

Kent looked to Eleni for confirmation, but she was staring at Ben, unsure of what to say. Kent took her silence as agreement.

"What else?"

"He said something to me," Ben said, now turning and facing Kent, this between the two macho heroes. "That was what really did it."

"What did he say?"

"Well . . . Ells had stepped away for a second, so she doesn't know this part. He said, 'Minute I get your girl alone, she's getting fucked whether she wants it or not.'" Ben glanced at Eleni. "'Doesn't matter how much she cries for you.'"

"Total jack-ass," Kent was saying, making a note.

"I just, I couldn't let that stand, you know?" Ben said. "I should've been calmer, should've called the cops, I guess, but then he's touching Eleni again, telling her to ditch me for him, and I'm scared, you know, for my girl. I didn't mean for it to escalate, but I wanted to tell him not to mess with her, so I followed him out . . . next thing I know, he's taking a swing at me, and I swing back, and I guess I swing harder than I meant to, and he's out cold . . ."

Kent nodded and gave Eleni a courtesy glance. "That sound right?"

Eleni shrugged. "It all just happened really, really fast. It was upsetting."

The drive back to the cabin was as silent as the drive the previous night, only the atmosphere was different now. Ben bristled with some kind of pride. He was somehow back in total dominance, and Eleni, whose help he'd desperately needed before, was now once again small, secondary. The pleading for her to understand why he'd done what he'd done was gone, along with his sweet tone. It was almost as if the whole thing never happened; that night, he expected things to go on as usual, with food and laziness and sex.

Even though Paul was still sitting in a hospital bed somewhere with the headache of his life.

Eleni suddenly felt awash in guilt, thinking about these things. She hadn't thought about that day at the police station since it happened; she'd forced it from her mind as soon as it was over. It was just another thing that happened to them, part of their story, their intensity. Part of his love, and she loved him in spite of it, and did that somehow make her more lovable, more perfect? Because that was what she wanted to be. He'd be more trusting, calmer when he saw how, over time, she hadn't let anyone else come between them.

She looked at her phone. Almost 3 a.m.

Something urged her to keep looking for a gun.

11

THE DISCOVERY

Thirty minutes later, Eleni's painfully heavy eyelids were drooping. Papers and memorabilia, taken out of their boxes, were in neat stacks on the floor. No gun. She probably should have expected as much. After all, the police had gone through every one of these same boxes. Would they have left a gun behind if they'd found it?

Aimee hadn't been killed with a gun, so Eleni didn't think it would have been considered evidence . . . although some theories suggested that her killer had held her at gunpoint or possibly threatened her with a gun, right before her murder.

If the police thought there had been a gun at the crime scene, then she supposed they could have taken it as evidence. It could be lying in a police station somewhere down in Oregon, where the case remained open, bagged and boxed in an evidence basement like she'd seen on TV. She rifled through some more papers, thinking of all the boxes in this loft as the "evidence room" of Ben's life and their relationship.

Theirs and possibly someone else's. She found a bunch of photos of a pretty brunette, sometimes with Ben in the picture, arm around her, sometimes not. An ex-girlfriend?

She gave up, shoving the photos back into a box. Looking down into the living area, she saw the fire had gone completely out. Where dying embers had cast a reddish glow just in front of the fireplace, there was now solid darkness. The lantern, glowing in the loft, threw a small amount of light down into the space below, but the dining area, off to the right, was lost in shadow. She squinted toward the corner where the wolf had gone, trying to see if there'd been any movement or change of circumstance. Everything was black and still.

She crawled back into bed beside Jacob, grateful to slide under the covers. Already half-asleep, she almost completely ignored it . . .

The clinking sound of a shifting stone.

Then, eyes shut, willfully trying to tell herself just to get some sleep, she couldn't un-hear it. At first, she thought, *There's just a loose stone in the chimney.* Then, *What if it falls on Jacob?* Her eyes pulled open. As she scanned the side of the chimney for the culprit, another thought crept into her mind.

She hadn't actually searched everywhere.

And neither had the police.

Ben had loved to leave her little notes around the cabin, things for her to find unexpectedly on days when he was gone for long stretches, out hunting or working some odd job in town. She'd pull out her suitcase to fish for a clean shirt and find a letter folded up there:

I'm missing you, miss. Miss—miss me!

Or *The love of my life, the lady of my cabin—can't wait to hold you again.*

She'd found notes in boxes of crackers, between the bedsheets, even in the freezer. Those little tokens somehow sustained the idea that it was ok—desirable, even—to be spending her days in a cabin with bars on the windows, where she didn't feel safe stepping outside alone because of the stories she'd been fed and the bears she'd spotted. On more than one night, half-asleep, they'd heard something outside and peered through the window to see a large grizzly sniffing around their porch, probably drawn to the scent of what was inside. It could be the scent of food cooked in the kitchen or—as Eleni often worried—their scent. According to a story that had made the rounds far too often, a woman in town had actually been chased up onto her roof and killed by a bear while she was on her period.

But all that faded away when Eleni felt loved, and she felt loved whenever she found a note. Once, she'd woken up to see a cut-out paper arrow pointing toward a section of the fireplace. Running her hands around the chimney, wondering what it meant, she'd found a loose stone. She'd pulled it out, and there was yet another note:

You're my rock!

So cheesy. So sweet. She still had that note, with a small stack of others exactly like it, back home. After finding it, she'd slid the rock, heavy, back into place.

And when it went back into place, it had made the same kind of heavy clink that she'd just heard.

She was sitting up now to see which rock had moved. The mattress must have pushed up against it, disturbing it, when she'd climbed back in the bed.

And there it was, near to the mattress. Almost unnoticeable, but there was a crack between this rock and the cement that filled the gaps between all the surrounding rocks. She reached out, touched it, shook it . . . and began to pry it loose.

Was it possible he still had a gun in the cabin, hidden in a secret hideaway like this? He'd built this place himself . . . he could have designed a small cubby, a place where he could stash something important—or dangerous.

As she dislodged the rock, her thumbnail bent back; wincing, she popped it forward again.

The rock was out and, with it, flecks of dirt and crumbled concrete. The light from the lantern didn't reach all the way into the hole. She fumbled her phone out of her front pocket, tapped the flashlight on, and bent to shine it into the opening.

There wasn't a gun . . .

But there was something else.

Squinting, bending, Eleni wasn't sure what it was at first. It was almost camouflaged by the dirt permeating its surface, having been between stones for who knew how long. She tentatively reached in, her hand braving its way past some dense, oily cobwebs, and pulled it out.

It was a stack of papers—*more papers?*—bound together so tightly and for so long in the pressurized little space that they had almost become one solid block. She pulled at the rubber band wrapped around them, and it broke, having solidified and glued itself onto the papers' surface, leaving chunks of caramel-brown stuck to the pages. As she got the pages to separate, some cracked and peeled, and she saw it wasn't just papers—there were photographs too. One photograph, stuck to the back of an envelope, had part of its glossy surface peel off as she pulled it away.

"Shoot," she whispered, trying to go slower, easier. She got the rest of the photograph off and gave it a quick glance. Then she looked again, holding her phone flashlight almost right up against the image.

It was flecked with brown spots, partially rotted. The pretty face in the photo had been slightly warped along with the paper, but it was a face she'd recognize anywhere.

It was Aimee Hart.

12

THE MURDER

Eleni stared at Aimee's image for a long time, examining every curve of the other woman's face, flecked though it was with partial rot from being entombed behind the stones of the chimney. She'd stared at that face before, in the newspaper, when the story of Aimee's strange murder had been national news. The story gained more traction when Ben, the prime suspect, disappeared, eluding authorities; instead of fading from people's memories the way a lot of murder stories eventually did, Ben's disappearance turned this case into something legendary. Suddenly, all over the country, people began calling in tips on Ben Wilton—and people in town had turned against Eleni with venom.

She could no longer stay out at the cabin by herself, unable to drive in and out of the almost non-existent wooded trail on her own, and she was temporarily forbidden to leave the state, so she'd come back and rented a room above a bakery in town that had been around since the Gold Rush. It had reportedly also housed a brothel upstairs back in the day. ("Rumor was the buns upstairs were hotter than the ones downstairs" was one of the jokes she had always told on her tours, and it had gotten laughs every time.) The landlady turned Eleni's application down at first, not wanting to be "mixed up with the law." She'd softened, though, at Eleni's tears and the fact this young woman couldn't find a place anywhere else.

Suddenly, everywhere she went, she felt eyes on her. Eleni had tried so hard for so much of her life to blend into the background and avoid conflict. On one trip to the grocery store, she'd stepped away from her cart to grab milk—and returned to find that someone had spit on top of her carton of eggs resting in the toddler seat. On another trip to the post office, walking down the boards of the sidewalk, someone had hissed "murderer" in her ear as he'd passed her, as if she had been the one to do those unspeakable things to Aimee. The glare in the cashier's eyes at the store did not escape her when she purchased a paper that bore Aimee's photo on the cover page. Eleni needed to read the latest details. She needed to look at this person she'd never met, who Ben said he'd never met, but who was now, somehow, a serious enough part of their lives that she carried more weight than most of Eleni's own relatives.

In that large, clear newspaper photo of Aimee's smiling face, she gazed into the camera directly. It was the best picture her parents had been able to find to give the police. Aimee was beautiful, with golden blond hair and a big smile full of even white teeth. She had a face that could pull off red lipstick. Looking now, Eleni noted Aimee had on the same red lipstick in the rotting photo from the chimney as in the newspaper photograph that had smiled back at her for weeks and weeks every time she was in the store. Police and publishers used it again and again; that picture became like a household name, instantly recognizable.

Eleni read about what happened to Aimee, and it was ghastly. She'd been taken to the woods in Oregon and raped. Her hands had been bound during this part of the process, and police speculated that she'd been bound before being taken to the woods. They also speculated her attacker had forced copious amounts of alcohol down her throat with the use of a funnel—not enough to kill her but enough to completely disorient her and make her attack seem that much more of a surrealistic nightmare. Trace amounts of drugs had been dissolved into the alcohol.

"She would have been alert enough to fully know what was happening to her but wouldn't have had control enough to fight back against her attacker," one police quote had read, going off the toxicology reports.

After the rape, Aimee's conscious, cognizant body had been toyed with in other ways. She'd been cut—again, not enough to kill her but just enough to cause agony and to make her fear levels spike. Police remarked that her mouth had been left ungagged during the whole process. There was no bruising about the mouth to indicate a gag at any time, leading them to believe the attacker had enjoyed listening to her pleas and screams as part of a power trip.

They assumed the attacker worked alone since all the bruising on Aimee's body matched just one size handprint. No fingerprints, though. There was only one set of footprints around Aimee's corpse when it was discovered (although those closest to the body, it was clear, someone attempted to cover up). In terms of the rape, forensics showed she'd only been violated by one person.

Police later told Eleni, off the record (it had been kept out of the newspapers, at first, for decency's sake, although later the media heard about it and rushed to publish a new slew of articles analyzing its meaning), that once dead, Aimee had been posed in an obscene manner, as if masturbating with her cold, dead hands. "A psycho like this," a cop had told Eleni, "the goal is to humiliate his victim to the very end. He saw that as a way to humiliate and shame Aimee Hart."

All of these peripheral tortures and embarrassments, though, were secondary to the main point: Aimee Hart had been murdered. And the thing that killed her, according to the autopsy, was not the forced alcohol and drugs. It wasn't the series of cuts that, yes, would have made her bleed but not enough to die. It wasn't the rape, although that had apparently been violent and bloody. It was the final act, after Aimee's torturer had had his fun, of proceeding to saw her head off.

Aimee had been alive when this process began.

So many nights, on her cot in the upstairs room at the bakery before she was allowed to leave Alaska, Eleni imagined herself lying prone on the forest floor. She imagined herself bleeding and nauseous, fallen pine needles pricking her skin. Imagined the onslaught of chemicals rushed down her throat via a plastic funnel that was shoved in her mouth so hard it scraped her trachea. She felt the jabs of the wood chips beneath her stripped, naked back (for Aimee had been stripped), watched blood spill from cuts in her skin and soak into the earth, then felt the full weight of a man's body as one of his knees knelt on her head, impacting her skull, before the teeth of the saw went into her neck and began to rake back and forth.

He would've been telling her what was coming. Listening to her crying and begging. Enjoying it.

But what else could she have done but cry and beg?

Eleni became obsessed with Aimee Hart. At one point, after she was allowed to leave Alaska, she even went to Aimee's hometown in Oregon and parked outside her parents' house, an aged, brick rancher with dark blue shutters. She sat there for over an hour, wanting to go in and talk, to tell them that she was so, so sorry for their pain but that it wasn't Ben who did this—it *couldn't* be Ben.

The newspapers also latched on to another figure—an uncle of Aimee's named Arlen. Arlen was a criminal with filed teeth who reportedly abused Aimee as a child and who, allegedly, she'd still been in touch with despite her parents' trying to cut him out of their lives. He apparently wasn't the type to be cut out. Eleni had seen a fuzzy picture of him in the paper as well, his teeth sculpted to points creating an unnerving effect on the front page. Didn't it make more sense, much more sense, to accuse this clearly unhinged individual with a history of violence and a fixation on Aimee than it did to point the finger at Ben?

At that point, Eleni was about seven months pregnant, stomach extending toward the steering wheel of the car. She'd sat and thought, sat and thought, watching the plastic rainbow pinwheels that had been planted in the mulch of the Harts' front flower beds spinning in the breeze . . . until, finally, Aimee's father came outside and, in a way that showed a straining for strength, walked toward her car.

"This isn't a museum; it isn't a roadside attraction," he said as if he'd already said it a million times. "You're upsetting my wife. Please, move on."

"I'm sorry," Eleni said, starting up her engine.

"You're all jackals!"

"I really am sorry."

He squinted at her then as she put the car in drive.

"Hey . . . you're—"

But she took off.

Later, a cop had come by the motel where she was staying for the night. She'd been easy enough to find.

"You can't go over there," he said firmly. "What were you doing there?"

"I just . . . I wasn't trying to make trouble for them. I guess I just wanted to see them."

Aimee's dad had recognized her from the newspapers, just as she had recognized him. A photo of him and his wife clutching each other for support at Aimee's funeral had run, and Eleni had stared at it, the anguish in their faces all too real. Apparently, they'd been scared that Eleni was in league with Ben, coming to threaten them or to make disparaging remarks about Aimee and all this being a set-up. To hurt them. She wouldn't have been the first one. Every town contained a vicious element who liked to hurt those in public mourning, regardless of the circumstances.

She realized that as much time as she'd spent studying Aimee's photograph, Aimee's parents had probably spent an equal amount of time studying photographs of her and Ben. Most pictures were only of Ben, but the papers had somehow managed to get ones of her too. Her name was given. People talked about the "girlfriend of the murderer." Aimee's parents had probably memorized the lines of her face; just as Eleni had stared at Aimee's face, wondering what it would be like to experience such torture, Aimee's parents had likely stared at hers, wondering what sort of woman could love and sleep with the man who had so brutally butchered their daughter.

But it wasn't him. That's all I want you to know. You're searching for the wrong person.

Police had simply come to question Ben at first, not arrest him. After they left with Ben in the back of the squad car, and as he underwent his first round of questioning, Eleni, confused, waited in the cabin. When Ben returned from the station, he explained to her that they had no leads and that cops always felt pressure from a town to solve a murder—especially a town as sleepy and tiny as the one Aimee was from, where nothing ever happened, and people became radical about their safety. Their links to Ben were flimsy at best; he had also lived and worked in that same town, right up until the time Aimee went missing. The day after her disappearance, he'd come back to Alaska, meeting Eleni only a week later. He hadn't been fleeing anything, he explained—the timing was just a coincidence.

There were rumors linking him and Aimee in a romantic relationship. They'd been seen at a local bar together, but as Ben told her, "There's one bar in that town. Everyone's there every weekend. We probably were there at the same time— doesn't mean we were together." There was a surveillance video of them going out the door together, but Ben said, "I was just holding the door for her. She wasn't a girl I knew. We might've made small talk; I didn't know her name." The bartender said they would sit together and talk and drink for hours, though, on more than one occasion.

"You know how it is, big groups hanging out," Ben said. "She was just there. I barely remember her because we barely spoke. Hell, I think the memories I do have are just from the cops telling me, over and over, that I saw her there. I don't even know if they're real."

These were the things Ben said over and over until Eleni saw the logic in them.

But now, here she was, with a picture in her hand . . .

And it was Aimee Hart, leaning against a body that belonged to Ben (though his face had been lifted off the photo, sticking to the back of an envelope in the pile). Aimee was leaning on him affectionately, looking up at him, one hand on his chest. They were standing in front of a picnic table by a lake, in the shade of a tree.

On a date.

Just then, Eleni heard it—

"Looks dark."

A man's voice. Just outside.

Ben.

He had come, after all.

She stuffed the picture back in the pile and shoved it all back in the chimney. The stone went in, not fitting as well as it had before. She didn't want him to know what she'd found.

The doorknob rattled, and there was banging.

"Get it open, will you?" came the man's voice again, muffled through the walls.

She reached out and cranked down the dial on the lantern, snuffing out the light.

Metal clanged against metal, then the deadbolt clicked aside as it was manipulated into releasing. The door swung open effortlessly.

Eleni crouched down low, putting an arm around Jacob, too scared to breathe.

There were three of them.

And they had guns.

13

THE BAD GUYS

As Eleni slid toward the back of the loft, it felt as if she was literally shrinking. Her shoulders collapsed forward, hunching, trying to compact her body. Her head came down with them, arching low. There was a feeling inside her chest of complete and utter contraction, a pulling in.

"The fuck happened here?" she heard as the sweep of a flashlight went over the room down below. Its beam momentarily cast up toward the ceiling and toward the loft. It hovered for a moment over the area where the ladder had originally been bolted to the wall.

For a moment, mind spinning, she thought they could be three rangers, or three police officers, come to check on her. But then she thought of their clothes; there was nothing official about them. Two of them feigned tough-guy personas in jeans and ratty coats. She hadn't yet gotten a good look at the one in the back.

"Something's gone down tonight, anyway," she heard another voice, followed by the sound of the front door closing again. A chair scraped against the floor to prop against the door and keep it shut. When the voice spoke again, she could tell the speaker had turned, now facing the one who entered last.

"You think he's already gone?"

There was a chill in the conversation as if waiting for this one person's answer had suspended every thought the other two men could possibly have in mid-air. When the third voice spoke, Eleni could tell there was something different about its personality.

"Are you suggesting that I won't get what I came for?"

"That's not what I meant. Just . . ."

The voice trailed off. Eleni, pressed almost flat to the ground beside the mattress, instinctively reached to put a hand on Jacob, who was still breathing steadily.

"That I should've done something differently?"

"That's not what I meant."

Footsteps moved back and forth across the floor. A light switch flicked up and down, to no avail.

"Get the fire going," the third voice, the in-charge voice, snapped at one of the others. "And see about getting the generator on."

Eleni pressed her face into the right angle created by the mattress meeting the floor, trying to calm her breathing. She heard one set of feet go to the kitchen and start to push back her pathetic little barricade.

"Come look at this," the voice called, and the steady feet paced into the kitchen. "The fuck did this?"

"All getting burned to the ground anyway."

The two murmured. Eleni half-heard instructions about shooting anything that moved, then setting the table back up when the guy got back.

Outside, a wolf howled. Confident, slow feet paced back into the living room to look out the window.

"I'll wear his skin before the night's over." Eleni couldn't tell if the man meant the skin of the wolf, Ben, or his own worker.

"Lead wolf out there," one of the other, lesser voices said. It sounded like the voice's owner was near the fireplace, trying to get it going. "Can tell by the tail. Lead keeps his tail up."

"How do you tell with men?"

Eleni's mouth was pressed so tightly against the mattress that the fabric felt damp. Her guess about how to tell with men was simply that they all had voices like this person's. The "in-charge" person's.

An orangey glow began to permeate the lower level.

"Check out what's up there," the steady voice came. She heard the broken bits of ladder being prodded, tested. Then she heard someone lift and drop her rope made of bedsheets. It thudded lightly against the wall.

She forced herself to move, but it was as if a ton of granite pushed down on her back; she didn't dare lift herself more than a few inches off the floor. Coming fully up alongside Jacob, she carefully pulled him to her, then slid back and away toward the back corner. She drew him into her lap, his head lolling, then went into a crouch as she came up against the wall. Her free hand strained to drag some boxes in front of them. She heard the destroyed ladder being moved against the wall and saw the top point of the still-in-tact side jerking back and forth in her field of vision.

The electricity flicked back on. The space heaters hummed.

"That's better."

She heard the heavy weight of a person step up onto the chair, still at the base of the wall. It was only a few feet before he'd be able to look at her, this lackey being sent to scope things out. He grunted, his weight seemingly up on the back of the chair. He pulled against the sheet, using the ladder post for some leverage.

She curled in as far behind the boxes as she could manage. Even so, she knew her back was sticking out, visible among the shadows.

"There was an animal in here tonight," she heard, and for some reason, she found herself hoping they wouldn't find the wolf, the wolf who would have been happy to eviscerate her only a few hours prior. At least the wolf acted on instinct.

But she could tell, in this person's voice, that he operated out of sickness.

Heavy breathing heaved its way up onto the loft floor. Sounds in the kitchen said the barricade was going back up now that the energy was back. Heavy footfalls got their bearings, only feet away.

And, of course, they came straight for her.

"Boss," she heard, although she refused to look up just yet. "We've got a surprise up here."

14

THE INTRODUCTION

The man who had come into the loft, a large, thick type in heavy boots and a black jacket, pulled away the box that Eleni had used to partially cover herself. As he did, Jacob came into full view, still sleeping, unaware, in her arms.

The man didn't hesitate. Hesitation would have implied a momentary pause of conscience. No, he only took a brief second to smirk, almost as if this innocent child made whatever was about to happen even more delightful.

"Make that two surprises," he called, keeping his eyes fixed on the mother and son. Eleni slowly, finally, looked up to see who had discovered her. His flannel shirt, visible in the gap of the unzipped jacket, strained across his barrel stomach. His face was covered with dirty blond bristles, his cheeks red and plump above the tree line of his would-be beard. The curls of his hair were greasy, clumped together with product that had been accumulating, never getting washed out before more was put in.

"Wilton?" Eleni heard from below, then the voice of the third man, the in-charge man. "What is it?"

"Not sure just what we have here," the man in the loft said, still looking down at Eleni. He was stooped over to keep from hitting his head on the ceiling, which made him look all the more menacing. Without any attempt at asking her to move on her own, he reached down and grabbed both the hood of her sweatshirt and one of her forearms, yanking her out into the small, open space in the center of the loft. The seam of the sweatshirt's collar pulled tight against her throat in a precise line, momentarily choking her while he dragged her from her hiding spot. Jacob was jostled roughly as she was pulled and opened his eyes. He gave a sharp, short mewling sound of complaint.

"What was that?" came from below.

"That was a kid," the thick man said, still seemingly deciding what the best, most enjoyable way would be for him to present this unfortunate pair. Eleni gripped Jacob tightly, still seated. The child pressed his head against her shoulder, still trying for sleep.

"A kid?" came an incredulous voice. Eleni could tell it wasn't the boss.

"That's what I said."

"By itself?"

"Nope," the thick man said, now eying Eleni more definitively. "We got Momma here too."

It was as if she could feel their smiles spreading, even without seeing them.

"Bring 'em down here," the boss said.

"You know how to use those legs or what?" the thick man said, kicking at her feet. She nodded. "Then stand the fuck up."

Eleni did, shaky, slow. The inside of her throat was scratchy from the momentary choking, and she felt like she needed to cough. She was afraid to make a sound, though, as if everyone was on a hair-trigger.

He shoved her, slightly, toward the drop into the living area.

She came into view for the two men below the same way they came into view for her—one shaky, slow step at a time. Then there they were: one to the left, the other to the right. The one to the left held a gun and wore the same kind of clothes as the man in the loft. The one to the right held some contraption she'd never seen before, but she immediately recoiled at the sight of it: two chunks of wood, each with long, sharp metal spikes pointing toward the other, were joined together by two foot-long screws, one on each side, an open gap in the middle. His clothes, though, had a hint of the ridiculous about them, almost like a nerdy church father on a trip to Disneyland . . . white-washed jeans from the eighties and a red-and-white striped shirt with a collar and three buttons up to the neck. White sneakers. If he'd had a coat, he'd shed it somewhere in the cabin.

She didn't yet dare look into either of their faces, but there they were.

And there she was for them: disheveled hair, ratty pajama pants and sweatshirt, red, raw eyes, and clutching a toddler in fuzzy, flannel moose jammies and red socks.

The visual definition of prey.

"Good evening, darling," the nerdy dad one said, whose voice and looks—as viewed in Eleni's peripheral vision—gave away the fact that he was a good twenty years older than the other two. "What brings you to these parts?"

Eleni didn't get a chance to find out whether she could bring herself to respond to him or, if she did, exactly what she would say. She didn't get a chance because the other man, the one to the left, the one with the gun, spoke.

"Eleni."

15

THE HOSTAGES

Eleni's eyes snapped to the other man's face. Whatever instinct had said about not looking them in the eye, another, greater instinct responded to the sound of her own name from a somewhat familiar voice. She saw who it was.

"This is Eleni?" the boss-dad said, amused. "You looked better in your newspaper pictures, my dear. Although, from the look of it—" he gestured to the blood-spotted floor— "you haven't had an easy night."

Eleni noticed he had traces of the wolf's blood on his fingers; he had bent to touch it, inspect it.

"So, did you kill the bastard?" The man behind her said, and Eleni became acutely aware of how easy it would be for him to shove her from behind right now, sending her and Jacob out of the loft and crashing down into unavoidable injuries below. That might make the boss laugh, but she couldn't believe it would make the other man laugh.

Mark. Mark, Ben's friend, the one who had stayed with them to go hunting. Mark, who had always been nice to her, a buddy to Ben.

What was this?

She stared at him, silently pleading for some kind of answer, her toes flexed down as if they could root her to the floor if she was pushed. Then, indeed, she was pushed—not

109

hard, not enough to go over the ledge—just enough to stumble forward a few inches, which felt massive in her current state of fear.

"Hand him down," the man behind her said, pointing to Jacob, then down to the others.

Mark glanced at the boss-dad, who gave a slight jut of his chin toward the loft. On cue, Mark stuck his gun through his belt and came to stand beneath where Eleni was swaying. He stepped up onto the chair.

"Go ahead, Mommy," the boss-dad said, and Eleni finally looked into his face, too, as if "Mommy" was close enough to her actual name to get the same result Mark had. There was something unsettling about his mouth, but it closed before she could put her finger on it. His yellow-white hair stuck out around his head, combed but puffy. He had a long waist, a torso that seemed almost too long for the legs below it. "All the good toys are down here."

She had seen this man before too. Where had she seen him?

The man behind her threw her coat down, then each of her boots. The coat landed on the floor by the boss-dad, buttons clacking against the floorboards. He lifted it and rifled through her pockets, which were empty except for some ancient, frayed tissues, a stray cough drop, and a few pennies. He chucked it on the bed.

She couldn't bring herself to move or speak. She looked to Mark again as if he could fix things. He was holding his arms up, waiting for Jacob.

The man behind her grew impatient.

"Hand him down before I fucking throw him down," he said, nudging her again. She stumbled another inch, then dropped to her knees, clutching Jacob in a bear hug, heavy tears suddenly falling from her eyes, even though she hadn't felt like she needed to cry. Mark locked his eyes on hers.

"It's ok, Ells. I got him."

She felt a boot press into her back, every defined ridge along the bottom of the rubber sole pushing into her. The foot was large enough that the heel ended in her lower back, but the toes landed up between her shoulder blades.

Shaking, she lowered Jacob toward Mark's waiting hands. Jacob's eyes fluttered open as he passed through the air, first hanging suspended from her hands, then taken into Mark's. He made a noise and looked at Mark, eyes still bleary. Then he looked up, and his eyes found Eleni.

"Mommy," he said softly, calmly. He seemed dumbfounded, trying to understand what he'd woken into.

Eleni felt the same way, but she also knew enough to be scared.

Mark got off the chair and paced away, her baby in his arms. Jacob seemed content to snuggle into him.

"Your turn," the man behind her said, giving one additional little shove against her back with his boot. Eleni, trembling, stood and made for the makeshift sheet-ladder.

"Pat her down first," the boss-dad said, and the large man beside her grabbed her arm. He pinned it behind her and choppily moved his free hand up and down her frame—lingering over certain areas of her body—before shoving her away with a curt, "She's good."

"Check him," the boss-dad commanded Mark, who ran a hand over Jacob's body to make sure nothing dangerous was hidden.

Eleni's eyes landed on the pack with Jacob's nebulizer.

"I need that," she said, not sure how to word it to sound more deferential, respectful. She was desperate to know what type of wording would get the response she wanted. "I'm sorry. It's just—it's my son's medicine."

"What's going on up there?" came the boss-dad's voice, almost in a taunting sing-song. The thick man looked at her incredulously, as if she got more entertaining by the second.

"You shitting me?"

She didn't dare make any sudden moves toward the nebulizer, but she shuffled her feet an inch closer to where it lay on the floor.

"Or you can bring it down. But I need it with me, in case he . . . he has attacks sometimes . . ."

"Said she needs her kid's medicine," the thick man boomed, loud to her ears. There was a long pause from below.

"Bring it."

Eleni moved as if to bend for it—but the man shoved her back.

"I'll get it," he said, and he moved for the bag. He lifted it and, first thing, pulled the knife out of the front pocket and looked at her.

"Keep it. Leave it. I just want the medicine," she said, quickly, panicked that she'd be punished for this. "I forgot it was even in there." He tucked the knife through his belt and continued to rifle through the bag, pulling out the face mask like it was an alien object.

"Sure it ain't some fancy breast pump?" He sneered, looking her over. She still felt the pressure over her body of him patting her down.

"It's a nebulizer. For asthma," she said, and surreally, she found herself reciting the same lines she'd spoken to other mothers at the park, ones with healthier kids. "He's too little to use an inhaler. This fits over his face—"

"I don't need you to take me to med school. Go on, climb down." He slung the strap of the bag over his shoulder and began crowding her once more toward the drop into the living room. Eleni took up the knotted sheet in her hands and tried to walk her way down, as she'd done earlier. This time, she slipped and hit the wall, banging her knee and drawing snickers, but she somehow still managed to hold on with her numb hands. Soon, her feet were on the floor.

"Mommy, ouch," Jacob said, watching her with fascination, his little eyes continually flitting from person to person, trying to understand how they fit.

"'Mommy, ouch.' I love that," boss-dad said. "Too bad for Mommy, right?"

Jacob stared at him, then held his arms out for Eleni.

"Mommy, hold."

Eleni looked to boss-dad to see if it would be all right. He grinned at her, lips closed, then cocked his head toward her baby.

"Go on."

She went to Jacob, hearing the man from the loft clop down to the floor behind her, and took her child tight into her arms. Turning, she tried to get her back to the wall right beside the front door so no one could come up behind her. They were all watching her, though, advancing toward her with ever-so-slight movements.

Her eyes went again to the bizarre contraption held by the boss-dad.

"So, Eleni," he said, and he showed his *teeth*.

And that's what did it for her—the teeth. Perfect triangles, all of them, filed to points.

Arlen.

"Stupid name, Eleni," he said like they were chatting at a party. "I remember thinking it when I read about you in the papers. What happened, your parents forget the M?"

Eleni had had a childhood friend who'd pointed out that her name sounded like three letters strung together—L.N.E. They'd spent more than one lunch period trying to come up with what the letters could stand for. One of the options had been "Lost, Not Erased." Eleni hadn't liked that so much, but she remembered it now, almost smelling the chocolate milk in her thermos as this man, much like a grade-schooler, said her name was stupid.

"You're stupid, everything about you's stupid, and I'm the only one who actually cares about you."

"Mommy, bad word," Jacob said, catching on to the "stupid," which she had taught him not to say. He didn't know enough to identify any other bad words the men might use.

"Aww, that's cute," Arlen said, moving closer. "What happened here tonight?"

Eleni swallowed and tried to keep her eyes on his eyes instead of his terrible, threatening mouth. She remembered reading in the paper how he had eight teeth on the top filed, six on the bottom. The effect of seeing them in real life, as opposed to on a grainy sheet of newspaper or an ad-ridden website, was jolting.

"A wolf got in," she whispered.

"Did it get back out?"

She nodded—yes—and didn't look toward the side table.

"Where's Ben?"

"I don't know."

"I don't believe you."

"He never came."

Arlen smiled. "You mean he left you here all alone in the big, bad woods?" He leaned in conspiratorially. "He must not like you all that much . . . *Eleni*."

She had just taken a chance. It had always been a chance; it was never certain that Ben would come. Maybe she'd never thought he actually would—maybe she hadn't even wanted him to. She just didn't want to wonder what if.

"Have a seat," Arlen said casually, backing off. He dragged the chair that had been pushed under the loft to the center of the room.

Eleni hesitated.

"Go on. I'll even let you keep holding your baby . . . Mommy."

Eleni sat gingerly.

"Lord knows I don't want to hold him," he added.

No sooner than Eleni sat facing the dining area, she felt ropes going around her ankles. She looked down and saw Mark kneeling beside her, his face etched with guilt. As he worked his way up, he wound the rope around her and Jacob, now sitting in her lap, binding them together and to the back of the chair. Jacob began to struggle, then cry. Eleni kept shushing him gently. She was grateful they were bound together.

"Tell us where Ben is, and you and your little boy are free to go," Arlen said, coming closer again. Jacob, furious and insulted by the ropes, buried his face in her shoulder.

"I really don't know. I was never sure he'd come."

"His friend in town was pretty sure he'd come."

"Chaz?"

Arlen smiled, shrugging. "Loyalty goes right out the window in the face of a bribe. He didn't tell us about you, though. Shame on him."

He then held up the contraption, its threatening, rusty spikes gleaming dully from the fire. The heat in the room had again begun to climb.

"Shame on you, too, if you're not telling me something now," he said, considering. Then, smiling with his sharp teeth, he asked, "Do you know what this is?"

16

THE MEMORY

Eleni was mute before the device Arlen held in his hand, this odd rectangular joining of bolts, wood, and spikes. She managed to shake her head no, and grinning with the filed bits of bones that were his teeth, Arlen knelt in front of her, almost like the duke in Cinderella, planning to ease her foot into the glass slipper.

"May I?" he asked, touching her socked foot. He guided it through the mouth of this small machine, the spiky teeth lightly scraping and snagging the wool. She felt the spikes touch down on her insole and move up to her ankle, where the tied rope prevented them from going any farther.

"It's really supposed to go all the way up around your knee," Arlen said with his head cocked sideways. His voice was so even and practical that he might have been a bored shoe salesman discussing the fit of a new boot. "I wouldn't want to undo my boys' work, though."

Eleni's eyes flitted up to the "boys," and she got to see their reaction to what was going on. The large one was watching gleefully, all but leaning forward and rubbing his hands. Mark had turned away, pretending to look out the window, but Eleni could tell he just didn't want to see what might happen.

They'd shared beers and barbecue together. He'd slept over, Eleni playing the quiet, obliging hostess as he and Ben talked and prepared to go hunt. Now, he wouldn't look her in the eye.

Jacob was working hard to twist his head to see what was going on.

"This will give you an idea of what it does, though," Arlen said as he angled himself closer. With one hand on each of the large screws, a screw on either side of the teeth, he cranked them inward. The teeth simultaneously moved toward each other and opened up—actually, three layers of teeth now spreading out and separating, pulled down the spiral of the screws. As they fanned open, they opened her skin like a surgical tool. She felt their points go painfully, if only slightly, into the flesh and tendons of her ankle, dotting her with open wounds. She inhaled sharply.

"It's called a knee splitter," Arlen explained, back to being a salesman, "but my guess is, it'll work just as well on an ankle." He turned the screws again, not as far as he had on the first go-around but just far enough for the teeth to go ever-so-slightly deeper. Eleni exhaled a choking cry. He only smiled at her, like they were chatting in a mall.

"Don't worry, Mommy," he said, showing his teeth again, horrible and slanting out from his sore-looking gums. "I'm not going to do it all the way. It's the devil to pry this thing off once it's fully on. I want it ready when Daddy gets here."

He said *Daddy* in a sugary sweet sing-song tone, leaning over to make enthusiastic eye contact with Jacob.

Eleni's eyes burned. The fire popped and crackled behind her. Her view of Arlen swam, awash in prickling tears.

"But if he's not coming . . ." Arlen said, his voice changing now and the salesman face falling. His cheeks were somehow both gaunt and flabby at the same time, elasticity going with age, so they hung slack. "If I don't get to use this on him tonight, I am going to use it on someone."

His eyes, first boring into hers, then shifted down slightly onto the back of Jacob's head as the child struggled to turn and see.

Arlen looked back to her.

"You better just hope it's you."

He only half-undid the screws, then yanked the contraption back over her foot, leaving ripped rivers in her socks that filled with scarlet pools. Eleni screamed without meaning to, gripping Jacob like he was a lifeline and could somehow pull her back to normalcy. Jacob squirmed.

"Too tight, Mommy!" he said to her, surprised. She forced herself to relax her hands, but they were trembling, the backs of them rubbing against the coarse rope that bound her. Her whole body shook, and she tried to breathe the pain away—but no. It never dulled; it stayed sharp and severe.

She saw her blood on the tips of the knee splitter's teeth and thought about the flecks of rust possibly entering her bloodstream even now. Arlen touched her blood, and it mingled with the wolf's blood that had already dried on his fingertips. He rubbed his thumb and forefinger together.

"Still warm," he told her.

Eleni shook. Jacob pressed his head into the crook of her neck, and she smelled his strawberry shampoo, which had come in a race-car-shaped bottle. She bent her head and buried her nose in his hair to breathe him in while she still could. She didn't see Arlen nod to the larger man, who then walked behind her.

"Now, all we can do is wait," Arlen said to her. "Wait and hope, sweet Eleni. Willie—"

He nodded at the large man out of her line of vision. Willie, she presumed.

"I don't want her staring at me all night."

Before Eleni processed what that meant, she felt something heavy and solid crack across the back of her head with a breaking sound. With a delirious sensation of diving headfirst into a black, bottomless cave, she lost all consciousness.

—⁓—

From the sensation of falling down, Eleni swam into the sensation of soaring up. She heard a roaring. Struggling to open her eyes, she wanted to be back in the room with the three men, where Jacob was now, more or less, alone. She couldn't open them, though. Her eyes fought her. The back of her head and neck were sickly warm, and it was somehow comforting, like a blanket. Dipping in and out of memories, she couldn't quite manage to put herself in the right spot in the linear time continuum of her life. She'd almost grab onto the present and then slip back again, landing on the wrong sensory experience, landing in swimming pools and her studio apartment and in bed with Ben.

Soaring up, then, with Ben, sunlight pounding through windows all around them.

In his seaplane.

They were fairly common in Alaska, one of the key ways to get around. She remembered working on the train and seeing a newspaper ad for a three-bedroom, three-bathroom house right on the water. It was only $25,000.

She'd been amazed, not sure how that was possible until she realized the only way to get to it was by seaplane.

To the back left-hand side of Ben's cabin, there was a dirt trail, only about a quarter-mile long. While walking on it in the summer, the thick greenery made it look like you were never going to arrive anywhere—you were deep in the wilderness, nothing but trees and mountains for hundreds of miles. Then, at the end, you emerged—and floating there, up against a rickety, short dock that Ben had also managed to build himself, was his seaplane: an eggnog color with three red stripes along its body and one long wing centered over the cockpit, sticking out on each side. It knocked lightly against the dock, the fjord gleaming behind it.

Eleni felt herself pulled along, up into the air, inside it, though she hadn't wanted to be inside it. Ben loved it, getting up and looking out over the sun-soaked mountains, dipping in and out of them. Eleni gripped the plastic strap over her seat.

So many times, up in the air. Ben joking, laughing. Eleni scared.

Ben showed her his gun; he'd brought his gun in the plane, and he pointed it into her face.

"I could kill you, dump you right out over the fjord, right here," he said, icy cold waters below, no human eyes for miles. "No one would ever know."

Eleni, scared.

Ben, laughing. Just a joke.

But not really.

He'd said it just to let her know that if he wanted to do it, he could.

Eleni kept soaring up and down, back and forth, lighting on different moments in her life, fighting to get back to the right one. Briefly, she forced her eyes open and saw through oval, half-open slits the inside of the cabin. She saw broken bits of ladder on the floor, furniture askew, everything bathed in orange light from the fire. Men rustled and scattered papers up in the loft. Her eyes shut, and it all swirled black again.

The next time she opened them, a good deal of time must have elapsed, though it felt like it was only one struggling moment. But now, everything was quiet and still. She couldn't see the large man, Willie . . . or Arlen . . .

But right in front of her, stationed there in the other wooden chair, was Mark.

17

THE TALK

Mark's arms were folded, his brow creased and conflicted. It was as if he'd been sitting a long time in mid-conversation, even while Eleni was unconscious, talking to her continually in his mind in preparation for the actual moment when he'd get to speak out loud.

Eleni's eyes opened, and they were already making eye contact. Only then did he look away.

She immediately looked down for Jacob, still curled tight against her, fastened there with rope. He was sleeping again.

"They didn't hurt him, did they?" she asked.

Mark shook his head. She could see Jacob's nebulizer bag thrown haphazardly on the table behind him, next to her mittens and hat.

Only then, after she'd done her two official "mom checks"—Jacob, his medicine—did she register her own current condition. The back of her head throbbed more violently than she'd ever experienced, as if a section of her skull had indeed been split, and all the blood in her body was rushing to gather around the wound.

She moved her neck gingerly and felt the partially dried blood at the nape of her neck crack.

"Where are they?" she whispered, more mouthing it than actually speaking.

"You ok? Maybe you should just . . . stay sleeping."

"Where are they?"

She was dizzy, disoriented. But she wasn't going back to sleep.

Mark inched closer, sighing as if beaten.

"Willie's in the basement. Arlen's sleeping." He jutted his chin over her shoulder, toward the bed behind her.

"Sleeping?"

"Yeah."

The lights were out again, although the space heaters were still glowing. Eleni figured they were keeping a low profile.

"What time is it?"

"It's tomorrow, technically," Mark said, looking at the still-dark windows. Exactly how much sunlight would they get this time of year?

"There are wolves in the basement," Eleni said. She wasn't sure why. It was like a half-hearted "gotcha."

"Not anymore."

She waited, thinking.

"They killed them," she said.

"Yes."

"The pups?"

"They were a nuisance."

She felt her fingers dig ever-so-slightly into Jacob's fleece pajamas.

"Is Jacob going to be a nuisance?"

"I think he's going to be a bargaining chip."

He saw her expression and waited.

Eventually, she swallowed.

"What is this?"

He sighed and looked down again, as if waiting to see how long he could let the silence last before she demanded an answer. Just as she said, "Mark," he spoke.

"You weren't supposed to be here. No one said you'd be here."

"Why are you here?"

Another pause. Another "Mark—"

"Do you know who Arlen is?"

Now, she paused. She did know.

"Ells?"

"The uncle of . . . that girl . . ." she heard herself say. She didn't know why she hadn't said "Aimee." It somehow seemed easier to refer to someone so brutally murdered as "that girl" than by her name.

"Right."

Eleni latched on to the character of Arlen once she read about him in the papers because he seemed like a plausible suspect, someone who really could have killed Aimee. It would have made more sense. Her uncle, who allegedly abused her when she was young, was involved in all sorts of bad stuff: drugs and more. He wasn't in the mob per se but the head of his own strange cult of crime and personality; he was an easy villain who made the story about Aimee all the juicier to the media. A larger-than-life persona, wrapped in a long-torso'ed, socially awkward body, with teeth he gleefully whittled into points.

"Why is he here?"

"He knows Ben," Mark said, finally meeting her eyes squarely for the first time since she'd woken up. "They worked together, Ells."

Eleni thought of Aimee's photo, sealed in the stone wall up in the loft.

"Then why wouldn't Arlen tell the police?"

"How much did Ben ever tell you about his time out of Alaska?"

Eleni shook her head.

"He was into some bad shit. He was working for Arlen." Mark looked over her shoulder again, toward the bed. "Arlen tells the cops he knows him, the cops figure out the kind of stuff he had Ben doing, they figure out what exactly Arlen does."

"What does Arlen do?"

Mark shook his head.

"Ben stole a lot of money . . ." Eyes on eyes again. "Right before he took off up here, before you guys met. You don't steal from a guy like Arlen. And then, Aimee . . . his niece and all . . ."

"Mark," she heard herself say before she even fully knew what the question coming out of her mouth would be. Then she didn't ask the one she really wanted to. "Is that what you're all here for? The money?"

"The money, sure, but . . . we're here to kill Ben."

"You too? You're going to kill Ben?"

"I'm here because I was told to be here. Not because I'm going to be the one to do it."

"Did you work with them?"

Short pause. "Ben hooked me up with some jobs. I'm here now because I know this place. I didn't get much choice."

Then, finally, the question she really wanted to ask.

"Do you know . . . know, for sure . . . that Ben killed Aimee?"

To speak her name aloud gave Eleni a strange sensation. She thought it a hundred times a day, but to give it voice was almost like sharing some terrible secret or a bizarre personal detail she had only ever thought to herself.

"I know they were together . . . I know he didn't treat her right . . ."

"But that doesn't necessarily mean he killed her."

"He lied about knowing her."

"But maybe because he was just panicked that he'd be blamed?"

Mark sighed. "I once heard him say he'd do it."

Eleni closed her eyes and breathed in Jacob's scent again, trying for calm.

"Why?"

"She'd pissed him off."

I never did. I never had enough of a personality to.
"*I like that about you.*"

Eleni's eyes were still shut, Jacob's hair tickling her nose as she bent her neck to bring her face to him.

"You have to get us out of here, Mark, please."

Her eyes were open, gleaming. Head back up.

"Please. I have my son here. He's just a baby, please."

"Ells . . . I always thought you were a sweetheart, you know, but . . ." Mark said, head shaking again, true remorse in his eyes as he shifted them away from her desperate face. "There's no way for me to get you out of here without all of us being killed."

18

THE CHOICE

When Eleni heard Arlen stir on the bed behind her, she couldn't help but wonder if he'd been awake the entire time, waiting the way predatory animals wait. The sound of his stirring coincided with the sound of Willie's heavy boots coming back up the steps, followed by the scrape of the wooden block table against the kitchen floor as he pushed it back against the damaged door.

"Damn lock on the cellar doors is busted," Willie called from the kitchen before coming in. He held a plastic, resealable bag of chocolate-covered raisins Eleni had bought the day before, shoving a fistful into his mouth.

"It hardly matters," Arlen said lazily from behind her. "We aren't trying to keep anyone out."

Willie nodded at Eleni. There was a smear of chocolate at the corner of his lips, making her think of a spoiled child.

"Good morning, Mommy."

Good morning. It was still black outside. If Eleni had been home, she would have been deep asleep, her body cherishing the moments until her alarm went off and she began the routine of feeding Jacob spoonfuls of oatmeal while simultaneously getting ready to go to work.

Now, all anyone at work knew was that she'd called out for the rest of the week.

Arlen's feet hit the floor behind her and paced closer, slow and deliberate. She felt her hair stir from his breath and pictured his pointed teeth near her throat. Then his hand clapped down on her shoulder—the shoulder Jacob wasn't resting his head on—in a way that was friendly and familiar. Like he was her dad, arrived to give her words of comfort after some disappointment.

"So, what remains now," he said, "is to figure out just what to do with you."

Willie dropped the raisin bag on the table, neglecting to seal it. For some reason, Eleni latched on to that detail, her heart in her throat.

"I, for one, feel like a sitting duck," he continued. She assumed he was making eye contact with Mark and Willie, respectively, based on the way the eyes of the other two flickered up to look behind her, then back to her. Willie crossed his arms, all business now, chocolate still tinting his mouth. Mark slumped forward in his chair, forearms on his knees. He looked up at Arlen as if the weight of his head was unbearable.

Eleni's own head was still shrieking, her thoughts howling and unfocused. She looked at the ground and saw a log from the fireplace lying there, a few scattered bits of broken bark on the floor around it. She figured that was what had hit her.

"So, we gotta make a choice. Not whether to stay or go, 'cause I'm ready to go. But who to take with us."

His hand squeezed her shoulder affectionately, then let go.

"I can't be lugging two hostages all over Alaska now."

Eleni's foot throbbed then, competing for attention with her head, and she remembered that it, too, was injured.

"So, the main question is, who is Ben gonna care about more?"

At that point, Arlen finally came around into her line of vision, smiling down at her benevolently.

"His lover or his child?"

He crouched beside her, putting himself at her eye level. His tufts of yellow-white hair were tousled from lying on the bed, sticking up severely in the back. He pursed his lips, again like a dad come to offer some words of wisdom during one of life's trials, and gazed into her eyes with seeming sympathy.

"Eleni. Darling," he said. "Did Ben ever actually care about you that much? Be honest now."

Her mouth hung open.

"Well?"

"We were in love."

"Years ago. And truly . . . was *he* in love, or was it just you?"

More and more, she wasn't even entirely sure it had been her at all. Or Ben. It had just been some elaborate trick, a play for control. A giving over of control in exchange for . . . what, exactly? What had she gotten besides Jacob, who Ben most certainly hadn't intended to give?

She didn't answer. Arlen considered, gave a little frown, and reached out to touch her neck. His fingers came away with bloodstains.

"I'm gonna need you to say something," he said.

"The one you leave behind," Eleni said, throat dry and voice cracking. "What happens to them?"

He raised his eyebrows, amused.

"They become a fantastic message for good ol' Ben, whenever he gets here. A calling card."

"How?"

Arlen inhaled, excited, like a teacher who'd just been asked a question on his favorite subject. "Well, what do you think is preferable? A bullet through the brain or leaving someone here without any means of contact and all those hungry wolves out there?" He nodded toward Jacob. "Do you think toddlers can go insane? Do you think yours would if he was left all alone in here? No mommy, no food, no water? I've always wondered that. Because kids that little, they aren't really sane yet to begin with, are they?"

He reached his red fingers toward Jacob's mouth and traced his lower lip, leaving a faint trail of Eleni's blood behind. Jacob twitched in his sleep, sucked in his lower lip, then pushed it back out. It was less red than it had been before.

"Could be the last sustenance he gets," Arlen said, his gaze level.

If they took Jacob with them and left her behind with a bullet in her brain or otherwise, at least her son would stand a chance.

She didn't let herself picture Jacob in transit with these men. The picture of him alone, starving and confused in the cabin, was too intense for her to think of anything else.

"His lover or his child?" Arlen asked, breathing in and out.

"Take Jacob," she heard herself say, then began to panic because it was maybe some kind of trick, some mind game. Maybe they'd take her only because she asked them not to.

The confusion of it, the not knowing the right thing to say, the how to get out, was the worst part.

Arlen raised his eyebrows again.

"You don't have to . . . I mean . . ." Mark said, and Willie and Arlen both turned to him, genuinely surprised. "I mean, whoever we leave . . . we don't have to, you know."

He nodded at her.

"Leave Eleni, just . . . you don't need any more bodies."

"Someone dies out here, no one's finding them for years. If ever," Arlen said. "Not unless it's Ben fucking Wilton who does the finding, and he can't say boo about it. All he can do is come after us for the other one."

"He can tell that friend back in town."

"The one who helped us earlier tonight, you mean," Arlen said, then waited a bit. "That is the one you mean?"

Mark slumped, silent again.

"Could just as easily leave two bodies here as one," Arlen said, his level gaze now trained on Mark. Willie snorted a short laugh, then reached for more raisins. "You got a crush or something, Mark?"

"Fuck no. No," Mark said, eyes darting to Eleni. "I just think, you know, be smart."

"And a live witness is smart? Open your mouth again; I'll turn this into a two-man job."

Mark was fully shut up at that point. He folded his arms and looked at Eleni, head tilted down again as if the weight of it were just unbearable. He didn't have the guts to stand up to Arlen. Eleni knew, with certainty, that she wouldn't have either.

Arlen turned his full attention back to Eleni.

"Ben can always find someone new to fuck. I'm sure he already has," Arlen said casually. "He can't replace a kid."

Arlen looked over his shoulder at Willie.

"Write a letter. We'll nail it to her chest. Let him know that if he wants his son, he's gonna have to come to us."

He leaned back to Eleni, stroked her hair, and said, "You sure will make a beautiful calling card."

19

A PLANNED MURDER

Once Arlen made his decision, things moved quickly. Eleni sat immobile as the men sprang into action around her.

As much as she understood what was about to happen—what they had said would happen and what they were preparing for—it was all too unreal to process. Her body seemed to process it far ahead of her conscious thinking. While her mind had to forcibly tell her she was going to be killed within minutes—and still didn't seem to believe it—her body took the information in on another level, jittery with a mad dose of stress hormones that suddenly flooded her system.

Willie scribbled his note. Arlen gave it a once-over, nodded, and set to work.

"Take the kid," he said to Mark before nodding to Willie. "You—hold her hands down once the rope's off."

Mark cut the rope from around her torso. Her ankles were still firmly fastened to the chair. He laced his fingers around Jacob, right below the toddler's arms.

"No—" She reflexively held tighter to her baby, breathing in his hair, his smell, feeling his warmth.

"Let go, Mommy. You don't want it to be both of you," Willie said, the almost sing-song quality of his voice paying homage to Arlen.

Mark looked her in the eye and nodded.

"I've got him, Ells."

She told herself to hand Jacob over. That was the command her brain gave. But her fingers still had to be pried back as Mark lifted her child from her, as if they refused to obey what she had told them. She knew she had to let Jacob go, because if this was it, she couldn't be holding him when they did it. He couldn't have that as one of his early memories—the feel of his mother's body convulsing, her arms tight around him, as her life was shot or stabbed or clubbed out of her. Her final, hooked fingertip lost its grip on Jacob's fleece, and he was in Mark's arms. Jacob's eyes opened, and he gave a shout to see himself pulled away from his mom.

Willie, kneeling behind her, grabbed both of her arms and pinned them to her sides. His hands were so large they practically covered the entirety of her biceps, the whole stretch of her upper arm. She could still flail her forearms, which was a pretty useless task.

"Please—don't let him watch," she heard herself saying. Her brain still lagged behind what was happening. Arlen walked around behind her again. She looked to the floor. The log was no longer lying there.

What would it feel like when her skull broke up into hundreds of tiny shards after repeated pummeling?

Last Christmas, she had dropped one of the Christmas balls while decorating the tree. It shattered into pieces both large and small. Some of them were so tiny that even weeks later, after sweeping the floor and going over it with a wet rag, she would walk across the floor in bare feet and feel one, like a fine, near-invisible needle, slip into her flesh. She'd feel it for a day or more but couldn't actually locate it to pull it out with tweezers. It was that small.

She'd warned Jacob to avoid that corner of the studio, and he obeyed, habitually playing in other "safe" areas.

Her fevered brain pictured that red ball, silver on the inside, when it first broke. How tiny, how fine, could broken bits of skull be?

Mark nodded and started to back away, Jacob now squalling in his grip.

Arlen, behind her, said, "Does she make the rules now?"

Mark halted. Glancing back and forth between Eleni and the man behind her—the man, presumably, warming up with the log like a professional baseball player with his bat—he made one final attempt on her behalf.

"It's just gonna make the kid hysterical," Mark said. His chin was raised as high as it would go as he tried to avoid Jacob swatting at him. "You wanna hear this screaming for the next couple days, however long it takes Wilton to catch up to us?"

What if he never catches up? Eleni thought. *What if he never even comes, never knows I died trying to see him, never knows that this monster has his child?*

"He keeps screaming like this, you won't even let him live long enough to get Wilton," Mark added.

There was a pause behind her, Jacob's shrieking wail filling the space between spoken language. Eleni shook like she never had in her life—so much so that she almost wondered if she was having a seizure. Willie's hands clenched tighter on her jittery arms.

"Wilton's just gotta think we have him," Arlen finally said. "If he winds up being too much trouble, we can take care of it."

And then Eleni heard it. Somehow, through her own hysterical breathing and the back-and-forth between killers, she heard that first warning catch in the sounds coming from her son. The sounds that let her know what was coming.

It took another couple of seconds for Mark to hear it, furrowing his brow and looking down at Jacob. The catch was becoming longer, more pronounced; it wasn't a hitch in the breathing but a long, ragged effort at breathing itself. Tears and snot still bubbled from Jacob's face, but he gasped through them, unable to calm them down entirely despite the new issue coming on fast.

"His asthma," she said, her voice pitching in a panic that was different from the panic she felt for herself. She knew if she were to die and Jacob were to have an attack with only these men here to fend for him, Jacob would die too. It didn't matter that they chose her. Jacob would die too. "He needs his medicine."

She jerked her chin and her forearms to the medicine bag on the table. Mark looked behind him. Jacob struggled for air, his head tossed all the way back.

"Please, he needs his medicine!"

Mark looked to Arlen.

"Oh, brother, all right," Eleni heard Arlen say from behind her.

Mark grabbed the bag and rifled through it.

"Give it to me! You have to know how to do it!" she shrieked, knowing if she could only do one more thing in her entire life, this needed to be it. It was a desperation greater than the one to live, just to take care of this one thing that could give her hope that Jacob would survive.

"Don't give her the bag, moron," Arlen snapped. "Look through it yourself, let her tell you what she needs." He bent over, pressing his mouth close to her ear. "I don't want any nasty surprises coming out of that bag."

"There's a face mask and—some medicine—you have to put the medicine in the little cup attached to the mask—then put it over him—"

Mark one-handedly fumbled out the mask, the medicine, and the little battery-operated motor. Then, with a look to Arlen—"Yeah, fine"—he passed them to Eleni. Willie loosened his grip slightly.

Her hands, trembling beyond her control from adrenaline and terror, tried to unscrew the cap on the cup and pour the medicine without spilling. A good splash of it went onto her lap, soaking through her pajama pants over her thigh.

If Jacob died in the throes of this attack, they would have murdered him. They would have killed her child.

Her fingers slipped, almost spilling everything out of the cup, but then the cap screwed on tight. She got it, and she handed it over.

Mark got the straps around Jacob's head, the child's ragged gasps for air making Eleni feel like she was the one suffocating. He was gasping and heaving, the sensation of a closing throat making him gag and almost vomit. White foam dripped from his lips.

"Breathe, baby, breathe, baby," she said. The others, thrown slightly off their game for the first time, only stared. "It's ok—you'll be ok."

It took a few minutes, as it always did. For a few moments, Jacob's head lolled back, his face up to the ceiling, his eyes glassy, and she felt a terrible certainty that he was dead.

But then he lifted his head again, making an effort to pull its weight back forward. The breathing was ragged, but quieter, and he looked at Eleni, reaching toward her with one hand that was continually opening and shutting, grasping for comfort.

She actually smiled, exhaled a chuckle, and closed her eyes, which released two fat tears down her cheeks.

"Go on," Arlen said, more annoyed than anything. "Take him in the other room."

20

THE MOMENT OF TRUTH

No sooner had Eleni breathed that sigh of relief and felt a warm reassurance pulse through her—*Jacob's ok!*—than the feeling was sucked right out of her as if by some vicious, surgical vacuum. Mark gave her one last, lingering look, then spun on his heel and went into the kitchen, taking Jacob with him.

Jacob, now exhausted and still with the mask on his face, no longer made any noise but kept looking at Eleni, over Mark's shoulder, as they disappeared into the shadows. As far as she knew, it would be the last time she'd ever see him.

She wanted to shout goodbye, but then she didn't want him to know what was happening.

He probably knew anyway.

There was a long, plaintive wolf's howl from outside.

"What a beautiful sound to hear at the end of your life," Arlen said. His hand brushed her hair, still loosely held by an elastic band but completely disheveled, back out of her face. He tucked it behind her ear and smoothed it—again, like a gentle parent. Then she realized that he was simply clearing it out of the way so he could have a clearer shot at the base of her skull when he began his work.

He pushed it all over her shoulder in one knotty tumble, yanking the elastic out altogether. She heard small popping sounds as several strands of hair were ripped from her head, and the sounds mimicked the pops from the fireplace.

"I got pregnant in this room," she heard herself say. As had happened other times that night, it wasn't a statement she had planned to make. She thought to herself that when someone knew they were about to die, perhaps it just opened up a floodgate of what they might say, all filters and regulations off, just a pure stream of random remembered experiences they wanted to state, share—the things that had been most important to them.

She thought she was much more eloquent internally than externally.

She could practically hear Arlen's eyebrows raise.

"Far as I can tell, it was the only significant thing you ever did, the getting pregnant," he said, thoroughly amused. Willie's arms tightened again on her biceps, as tight as they'd been before giving Jacob his medicine. Eleni knew that meant it was getting close. "World shouldn't miss you all that much."

"But he will. He'll miss me," Eleni blubbered, feeling a draft on her exposed neck. She knew with certainty that, however little she might matter everywhere else, there was one person to whom she mattered greatly. And she had failed him.

"Benny-boy?"

"Jacob."

She heard a snort behind her, a laugh.

"Kids forget."

"Kids *remember*," she snapped at him, with true venom, the purest, angriest thing she could ever remember saying. "Kids remember every damn thing you ever do."

"And what idiotic things do you think he'll remember about you?"

Arlen was like a kid who liked to play with his food. He was a condescending parent and a spoiled, aggressive child, all wrapped into one.

She could only think of one out of the thousands.

Please don't take my sunshine away.

"You know," Arlen said then, switching tactics. She heard a slight thud on the floor, as if whatever blunt object he'd been getting ready to hit her with now had one side lowered to the ground, the other still grasped in his hand as he relaxed for a moment. "Parents remember everything too. You know that, don't you? I bet you remember every little thing about your boy. Every asthma attack. Each and every tooth as it came in. First time you heard 'Mama.'"

Where was this going?

"Aimee's parents remember everything about her too. They're fucking tortured by it. They've got Aimee ghosts all over their shithole town. And while they were identifying her body and putting those chopped up little bits that had been their baby in the ground, you were up here, fucking her killer. Getting pregnant."

She shook her head side to side on her thin little neck.

"Don't you think they should have justice?"

"I never knew Aimee."

"You said he didn't do it. I heard you. On the news. You defended him."

Eleni sniffed, snot clogging her nose from so much crying.

"Do you still defend him, Eleni?"

He lifted the object again and rested it on her shoulder, nestling it against her sweatshirt collar. The rough bark of the log pricked into her skin.

"You think someone's baby is any less their baby because she's grown?"

"We don't know it was Ben."

"I know it was Ben."

"You raped her," Eleni heard herself say, that about-to-be-killed, almost-dead, non-filter kicking in again. "Heard that on the news too. Her parents don't even speak to you. You raped Aimee when she was a kid. Police found it in her journals."

The heavy weight of the log lifted off her shoulder.

"Only someone who knew she was about to die," Arlen said, "would say that."

She felt the air rush around the log as it was pulled back sharply and braced herself.

And then Mark was suddenly calling out in a panic:

"Arlen! There's someone out there!"

21

THE HOMECOMING

The log was lowered once again.

"You shittin' me?" Arlen called.

"No. Fuck, come look."

"If this is some bullshit just to . . ."

Arlen stomped past Eleni in her chair. Willie's hands relaxed a bit again but still firmly held her arms.

"Well, I'll be," Eleni heard from the kitchen. "What a coward. Willie!"

Willie stood behind her and took up the rope again. He looped it tight around her, just under her breasts, and then once around her wrists, which he brought together at her lower back, behind the chair.

"Aren't you the lucky one?" Willie said, grinning in her face before getting on his feet and going into the kitchen.

They weren't watching her. She didn't know what to do with the momentary opportunity; she only knew that it was one. Pushing against the ground with her socked feet, she made the chair wobble slightly, then slide a few inches over the floorboards. Her hands flailed, bound together at the wrists, willing the rope to loosen. She looked around desperately—and saw the small hand axe by the fireplace. One of these men had found it and put it there.

Arlen was striding back into the room, arms flung wide.

"'Journeys end in lovers meeting!'" he said, grandiose. "Eleni, your journey is about to end, and it looks like you'll meet your lover after all."

She heard the table being pushed away from the basement door, followed by Willie's heavy steps going down.

"Ben is here?" she asked. "He came?"

"Let me ask you, knowing all you've been through tonight to see him: how does it feel to know he peeked through the window, saw your predicament, and tried to run?"

Once the sound of Willie had faded down the steps, everything went silent for a few minutes. Then shouts could be heard. She heard Ben's voice; she was alert to it in a special way, like a dog that could pick up on a certain frequency. They could have been in a crowded room, and she still would have detected that voice on the other side, distinct with his own inflections and expressions, like a fingerprint.

Then she heard a gunshot. She flinched against her soreness, then waited, breath held tight in her chest. Arlen and Mark waited too. Then, a few minutes later, there was the sound of scuffling footfalls as Willie forced Ben through the cellar doors. The rusty creak of the doors being pulled shut, despite the fact they couldn't lock, reverberated up into the kitchen, followed by more scuffling coming up the stairs.

"I'm going! Fuck, I'm going," she heard Ben say. "Think you ruptured my fucking eardrum."

The footfalls were then on the kitchen linoleum, so close, and then, with a shove, Ben's body was pushed into the orange light from the fireplace, into the same room as Eleni.

One side of his face was lined with blood, a hand clapped over his ear. As he lowered the hand, Eleni saw the cartilage of the ear was fringy. The bullet, presumably fired near his head as a warning, had just barely caught the curve of the ear's flesh and turned minute bits of it to shrapnel. His clothes were dirty, as if he'd been trying to crawl away on the forest floor. A few fallen pine needles and decimated leaves clung to his heavy coat. Willie now held an extra gun, Ben's gun, in the hand that hung down at his side. His other hand was still raised, pointing his own gun at the back of Ben's head.

Ben saw her, and the wince on his face loosened, then fell apart altogether as he looked at her in amazement.

"Eleni."

She stared back at him.

"You came," he said.

"For you."

He winced again, not for himself this time but for what he saw.

"You're hurt," he said, and his expression mirrored to her just how badly hurt she must look.

They're going to kill me stayed lodged in her throat, under the sob she choked down. *They're going to kill all three of us.*

Ben's eyes scanned the room and landed on Mark holding Jacob.

"Byrnes?" He spat, incredulous, before focusing on the child, who still wore his nebulizer mask. Ben looked back to Eleni. "That's my boy?"

He smiled a sad, tragic smile, teeth flashing in the orange glow. Despite everything, he was still handsome, even if he was thinner from being on the run with no money. Thick stubble now coated the lower portion of his face, whereas before, he was always clean-shaven. The stubble was peppery, with lighter patches here and there, gray and silver despite Ben being barely thirty. He looked much older than he was, but still . . . handsome.

"Your son," she whispered.

"What happened to him?" Ben asked, referring to the mask.

"Check him," Arlen said from behind her, referring to Ben and not Jacob. Willie went to work, patting Ben down. He pulled a long, dangling keychain from Ben's coat pocket, with a small rubber fish on one end and two jangling keys alongside a bottle opener on the other.

The keys to the seaplane. Willie threw them on the table. Eleni watched the light play off their silver edges.

Is that how he'd evaded capture all this time? Flying up into no-man's land, over the Alaskan wilderness, stopping only in the most secluded, deserted spots? Or had the plane been stashed somewhere for months on end, just waiting for his return, for the next time he'd want to come to the cabin and experience anything of the life he'd known before being wanted for Aimee Hart's murder?

A few other things were pulled from his pockets. A switchblade. A small cardboard box of bullets; damned if Eleni knew what kind they were or what kind of gun he had. It all went onto the table. An orange bottle of prescription pills with no label rattled when Willie pulled it out, and Willie smiled and tossed them to Arlen. "Yours if you want 'em." Willie pulled the thick coat from Ben's shoulders, leaving him in jeans and a long-sleeved t-shirt, looking much like the rest of them. If not for the guns, it would almost seem like Ben was just some guy who had come to play poker.

Willie tossed the coat to Arlen, who gave it a once-over, then threw it on the bed along with the pills.

"Don't try anything," Arlen warned Ben, and Eleni assumed he was still holding the log. She wondered where the knee splitter had gone.

"I'm outta moves," Ben said, mostly to himself. Eleni's eyes were glued to him. She glanced over at Jacob, who was also watching Ben in fascination from behind his mask.

"That's Daddy, sweetie," Eleni said, suddenly as exhausted as she'd ever been but full of tenderness. Would Ben get to hold Jacob even once before they were killed? She looked at Mark, jutting her chin toward Jacob's mask. "You can take that off now."

Mark did, throwing the entire nebulizer contraption back onto the table, now crowded with various artifacts from Ben's pockets and Eleni's own hat and gloves. Jacob gripped Mark's shirt in his chubby fists, having gotten used to being held by him.

"Daddy," he said. "Hi, Daddy."

"Hey, buster," Ben said, managing to give Jacob a bright smile despite what was happening.

Eleni felt her heart fill, thinking maybe, just maybe, Ben was innocent of everything, after all. That he'd, of course, been set up by this horrible person standing behind her, this person so clearly deranged and dangerous, who'd been sexually obsessed with his own niece. Ben knew them, sure. He had reasons for not admitting he knew them because maybe he'd done something illegal just to make some quick money—something he regretted. He'd run because he didn't want to go to jail forever for a murder he didn't commit. Sure, he had his flaws: he'd been with a dangerous crowd, and some of that had carried over into his personality. Into the fight with Paul. But he was good in his heart, and he loved her, and he loved the son she'd borne, and if they had to die, at least they were together, as a family, even if just for this once.

She could make herself believe it all so quickly, so easily. The key to how easy it was to believe was how much she wanted it to be true.

"He might've lived a few more days, your boy," Arlen said. "If you hadn't shown up."

Arlen, still behind her, must have made some sort of gesture because Willie then forced Ben into the other chair, pulled opposite Eleni, and tied him there.

"We're going to have a lot of fun tonight, you and me," Arlen said. "I've got a lot of surprises for you."

22

THE SCAPEGOAT

"First of all, don't you want to tell poor Eleni you love her?" Arlen said mockingly, jovial again. "She's been through a heck of a lot tonight, Ben, all because she wanted to see you. I can see why you liked her in the first place; she's a perfect little rag doll, isn't she?"

Eleni and Ben looked each other squarely in the eye, not speaking.

"Could put her through all sorts of shit before she said boo. That works out great for a guy like you, doesn't it? A guy who likes to control his girls?"

"Arlen," Ben said, finally speaking. "About Aimee—"

"We'll get to Aimee," Arlen said, leaning on the back of Eleni's chair so it creaked. "What I want to know first is, where's my money?"

"Your money?"

"Aimee's gone. And I'm pissed as hell about it but can't reverse the rotting process. She's gone and cut up, and worms are wiggling through her right now, far as I know. But the money? Now, that's somewhere. And I know for sure you haven't spent it—at least, not much of it—cause that would've made you easier to track. So, where is it?"

Ben looked down to the floor, searching.

"Where is it?" Arlen repeated, still in a normal tone. Then again. "Where is it? Where is it? Where IS IT?"

On the last repetition, his voice rose to ear-splitting volume. He rocked Eleni's chair to the side and let it drop back down with a bang, then charged forward toward Ben.

"The gunshot make you totally deaf?"

"I don't have your money, Arlen."

"Bullshit. I know you walked out with it; I got it on camera."

Ben looked over at Eleni, and his eyes fell to the floor, ashamed.

"It wasn't for me."

"What, you give it all to charity?"

"I walked out with the wrong bag that day. I never meant to take it."

Arlen turned to Eleni, incredulous. "Do you hear this shit? These kinds of psychos, they truly will say anything to dance their way out of trouble. Even when they know you know they're lying! Just throw a bunch of nonsense at the wall and see what sticks."

"It's the truth," Ben insisted, so Arlen turned back to him. "I was gonna bring it back that night, but then I got word of Aimee, and I knew how it was gonna look, and it wasn't me, Arlen. You would've killed me, and it wasn't me."

"Ok, hotshot. So, if it was an accident, and you haven't spent it, where is it?"

"I came up here . . ."

"Yeah."

"Well . . ."

"Where the FUCK is my money?"

Ben took the calm, measured breaths of someone who knew what he wanted to say but who was debating whether or not to actually say it. Jacob gurgled in a cute, baby way behind him. The gurgling took on a serious note that was slightly comical, and the sound, almost synonymous with innocence, made Ben flinch ever-so-slightly.

Arlen pointed his gun in Ben's face. "You don't have any answers. You're not good for anything."

"It's not that . . ."

Arlen stomped back behind Eleni, snatched something off the bed, and came back into view. This time, he was holding the knee splitter.

Ben straightened in his chair but didn't ask what the crazy contraption was. He recognized it. He had seen it before.

"You don't have to—"

"Apparently, yes, to get you to talk."

Willie was back to doing what Eleni discovered was a core part of his job description: untying and holding still body parts that Arlen wanted to hurt.

One of Ben's feet was now out of its shoe, gripped in the other man's hand.

"C'mon, for fuck's sake—"

"This is a really simple question, Ben. Really easy. You walked out of Oregon with over two million dollars. I don't think you left it on a train somewhere. Where is it? Is it here?"

Arlen handed Willie the knee splitter and stayed standing, looming over Ben, gun still in hand. Ben struggled against his ropes, panting.

"Is it?"

"Eleni took it home with her," Ben spat out. "She had it down in Washington."

Arlen's head swiveled slowly on his neck to look at her. The shock on her face registered with him immediately, and as if he had become her own ventriloquist dummy, he said, "You're lying."

"No, it's the truth. Baby money. But don't take it out on her—she didn't know all the background. She just found it when we were here, talked me into keeping it. Said it was all safe now, no one was chasing me. She had it; she's spent it."

Arlen looked at her again, raising an eyebrow. "That'd buy an awful lot of baby wipes."

"You know how moms are with their kids," Ben said, sweat visible on his face. The knee splitter had worked its way up to his left knee, much higher than it had been on Eleni, having tugged and frayed his jeans here and there along the way. It made her think of the garter at a wedding. She remembered catching the bouquet once, and some guy she didn't know catching the garter. He got it up to about her knee, then asked the delighted crowd, "Every inch above the knee's five years' good luck, right?" before proceeding to push it roughly up her thigh, under her skirt.

And she'd smiled and played it off, not wanting to spoil everyone's good time.

Like the idiot I am.

And then she thought, *Not an idiot. A polite person accommodating a jackass. Accommodating someone who didn't deserve to be accommodated.*

Her blood still rushed in her ears from what Ben had said, and yet that nighttime wedding was the memory that was somehow pounding through her heart, pumped out and recycled with every beat, infuriating her further. Whatever invisible floor had been beneath her heart up until that moment, holding it up and holding together what her life had been to that point, dropped out. All reason, all way of making sense of things, of framing this relationship in a way she could live with, dropped out with it, heart and soul tumbling over each other as the floor vanished and they plunged into nothing.

"What do you say, Eleni?" Arlen asked, still smiling. "Should the knee splitter be on you, after all, and not on Ben?"

"I'm sure you're gonna put it on me anyway," she said, her voice hollow and zombie-like. "Cause what am I here for if not for you all to just beat up on, tear apart?" She glared at Ben. "It's all I'm good for."

Arlen loved it. "Let it out, rag doll," he said, jubilant. Eleni started to laugh, to go crazy, and she could feel it, rocking in her chair—the madness that was now moving her flesh.

"Little Red Riding Hood, does the grandma let the wolf in?" she asked, smiling at Arlen, as if somehow, in that moment, he was her best friend, the person who understood her most, because he was crazy too. "Did she let him in, or did he break in? Cause you, you all broke in, each of you new guys." She looked around. "But you," she spat at Ben, "you, I let in. I let in. I let you in," and she had, like it was nothing, like there was no value to her at all, no value to the future children that might come of it. She was laughing and rocking and then sobbing and then just screaming and screaming and fighting against her restraints.

"Shh-shh-shh," Arlen was soothing her, stroking her hair back. "Feels good to yell, I know, but don't forget little one over there."

He pointed toward Jacob with his gun, and Eleni heard herself say:

"Don't point that at my child."

Friendship off the table.

Jacob was, indeed, watching her with wide, surprised eyes as if she were a stranger.

She hardly knew what was happening in this moment, when crying for help turned into a battle cry.

"Don't care if I have to chew through these ropes. You hurt him, I'll make your fucking knee splitter look like a kiss goodnight."

Arlen was starting to look annoyed.

"Know how stupid you sound right now?"

She did. Like every bad movie cliché she used to make fun of was clamoring over her tongue and out her mouth. She wouldn't make fun of them anymore because she knew the feeling behind them was real, even if the words were ridiculous. Those clichés at least conveyed the core of that feeling, however predictable.

"You'll be dead five times over before you're out of those ropes. And if I wanted to kill your son right now, I could."

"That's your misfortune," she said, not even sure what that was supposed to mean. She was now truly leaving the realm of sense.

"I know," Arlen said, now leaning in, picking up his sympathetic tack again. "Ben's just a horrible person, isn't he? Would it make you feel a little better—and maybe like being more polite—to watch me break his knee?"

"All I am is polite," she muttered, then slumped forward, the momentary burst of fury having pulsed its way through her and out. Like a leech had passed through her heart and taken all the blood.

"That's how you get taken advantage of."

"No, it's not. No, it's not," she said because she knew it wasn't just being polite to the undeserving that could undo you. Not by itself.

It was expecting someone else to come along and fulfill you, fix your life for you. Give you validation. It was letting someone else fill in for the personal power you were supposed to have instead of building it up yourself.

That's when the bad guys came.

23

THE BROKEN KNEE
(AND THE BROKEN BACK)

As her outburst subsided, Arlen lost interest in her, turning again to Ben. She wondered how many times this bizarre, wolf-like man had played out scenarios similar to this one, with people who had wronged him or with people who were only innocent bystanders. Was it like a theatre of the living to him?

"So, Ben," he asked, "don't you feel bad for Eleni at all?"

If not for the ropes and the blood and the fact her mouth suddenly tasted like metallic vomit, Eleni would have thought Arlen was some sort of deranged marriage counselor, prompting them to go over feelings and thoughts, prompting Ben to acknowledge exactly how he had treated this sad little life partner of his. She laughed again, picturing Arlen in a posh counselor's office, a couple in front of him, as he pulled out ropes. *Now, my approach is a little unorthodox, but all the couples I've worked with swear by it.*

The knee splitter, fastened over the top-half of Ben's knee, drew spots of blood at the base of each spike. Drops soaked through his faded jeans, and she heard how his breathing had slowed and deepened as he worked his interior system against the pain.

Answer, Ben, answer, Ben, her brain was in sing-song, loopy. She looked up and gave Ben a ghastly smile, but then her eyes landed on Jacob, and she tried to take a page from Ben's book, slowing her breathing. She couldn't lose her mind, and if it was already half-lost, she had to retrieve it. Because whatever happened, she needed to summon whatever she could within herself to help that small boy, who alternated between trying to pull one of Mark's buttons off his flannel shirt and looking to her for emotional reassurance. He was the only thing in here worth saving and the only thing she should ever have cared about. She nodded at him and pursed her lips to erase the ghoul's smile she had given Ben. When they un-pursed, her smile had somehow been molded back into something more regular, more comforting.

She didn't yet know what she was going to do, only that she was going to do something.

Arlen knelt before Ben, as if to propose. He put one hand on either side of the knee splitter, prepared to turn the large wooden screws. Eleni's eyes were again on Ben's face, this time serious. She was reading the fear she saw there.

"Last chance, lover-boy," Arlen said.

"I don't have it," Ben whispered.

Arlen turned the screws.

—m—

The screams were so horrific, so terrible, that Mark rushed from the room with Jacob without waiting for Arlen's permission. He pressed Jacob's left ear against his chest and covered his right with one of his hands.

"You're gonna upset your boy," Arlen said, then twisted again.

Eleni watched. All her senses were heightened. Ben sat at least eight feet away from her in his chair, but it was as if she could see droplets of blood entering the fibers of his jeans before they even soaked through. In his screams, she could

158

register octaves she had never heard before, nuances, like each individual moment was communicating different notes of the pain, each distinct and crystallized. She saw every pore on his face as it contorted and reddened, every draft in the room as it stirred the hair on their heads.

And she could see something unexpected.

The tablecloth in the corner, where the mother wolf had taken cover to lick her wounds, moved, rocking forward as if on the back of a creature who had risen and readjusted itself. It lifted outward, only a few inches, then fell back down again, and no one else saw it but her. Only her.

You're not dead. Neither am I.

Lost, not erased.

She didn't wince once, not even when she heard the loud, sonorous *pop* and knew Ben's knee had been broken. The spikes, deep into him now and fully spread, hadn't only cut through the muscles, tissues, and ligaments; they had also dislocated and displaced them, sliding broken flesh and bone under the kneecap, turning it all into a mangled ball of debris where Ben's knee had previously been. She didn't wince, didn't cringe. Oddly calm, she stared out at the room as if it were a vividly colored painting, awash in fire glow and agony.

"Perhaps . . ." Arlen said, standing and putting a finger to his lips. He waited for Ben's wails to subside long enough to know he could be clearly heard. "Perhaps I'm going about this the wrong way. Do you think I'm going about it the wrong way, Ben?"

A true tormentor pretended as if they were giving you a choice, Eleni thought. *They pretended it but knew they had the choice all along. They were in control.*

They can only torment you if they're in control.

"Perhaps you can actually settle a little debate we were having earlier this morning," Arlen said. "Mark, bring the boy back in!"

After some shuffling in the kitchen, Mark returned. Jacob clutched the plastic truck toy Eleni left in the kitchen earlier, the one she bought at the grocery store. She'd heard Mark discover it and wave it in front of Jacob's face, cooing, even over Ben's howling—when she'd been able to hear and see and sense everything.

"We were trying to decide whose life you'd actually value more, Jacob's or Eleni's," Arlen said. "We've already seen just how quick you were to throw Eleni under the bus, so I think that answers that for us. As it should be, right, Eleni? A parent's first priority should always be his child?"

He looked at her, waiting for her to grant permission for whatever upcoming tortures he had on his mind.

She had things on her mind too.

"Of course, Arlen," she said, and something in her voice gave him, the unpausable, pause. But he continued.

"So, maybe I'm going about this the wrong way," he said with a flourish, spinning as if presenting to a room of investors. "Because Ben didn't talk when he was being tortured. And we can be pretty sure that the threat of something happening to Eleni wouldn't make him talk. But of course, we haven't tried the absolute answer yet, and that answer is this fine little fellow right here."

He tweaked Jacob's chin, actually tweaked it, leaving a spot of blood on the child's jaw. Blood that had come from his father's knee when it dripped onto Arlen as he worked the knee splitter. Jacob looked at him in amazement. Eleni wondered if Jacob was transfixed by Arlen's teeth, trying to understand why they were like the big, bad wolf's.

"You won't talk when your own well-being's at stake, but what about his?" Arlen said. Ben looked up at him in a hang-dog way, mouth open, still recovering with heavy breaths. "I mean, I know you've never even seen this child before, never even held him—and you're never going to—but there's gotta be something instinctual in a parent about protecting their kid, right? So, let's see. Bring him over here, Mark. What's the best way to kill a toddler?"

Eleni felt her strange calm flicker as violently as a flame in a storm. But she reached out and caught it again, out of necessity.

"I think I have something better," Eleni said. "Something you'll enjoy more."

Arlen turned back to her. She was interesting again.

"Is that so?"

"You always have Jacob as a last resort," she said, her calm actually pulsing through the room and filling it. There was a power in the calm, and the whole room was suddenly on hold for her, the smallest one, broken and bleeding and tied down.

She was in control now, however fleeting that control might turn out to be.

"I think we're at the last resort," Arlen said.

"Don't you want to see just how much punishment I can take first?" she said, and she smiled at him. "You kill Jacob, he's so small and frail . . . and with his asthma . . . it will be over in minutes. But you come here, to me, you get to experiment."

"No Mommy say," she heard Jacob say, faintly, in the background. This was his simple phrase for whenever she said something he objected to. *No Mommy say*. She wasn't sure if the part that bothered him was hearing "kill" right next to his own name or if it was putting herself in jeopardy. She didn't look over at him—she kept looking at Arlen.

Arlen's eyes glinted.

"And Ben," she said, her voice regal now, positively in charge. "Bad enough you torture him. But the visual of what you can do to me . . . of me lasting through it . . . you'll make him sick to his stomach at the least, and I know you'll like that."

"He wasn't so squeamish about what he did to Aimee."

"When he killed her, he didn't know he'd be next. He only cares when it's going to be him."

Arlen cocked his head.

"I can still kill your son and have fun with you after."

"Oh, but . . ." She chuckled. "You won't have fun then. Because then, I won't need to survive. And I won't."

"You don't choose how long you survive. I do."

"You're wrong," she said, mocking him. "I can survive if I think there's a reason. Right now, there's a reason. And I can sit up and look you right in the eye as you do your worst, and we'll see how good you are, if you can make me scream. But you kill Jacob first, and I'll be a screaming, sobbing, wailing mess that'll find a way to kill herself if you take too goddamn long."

Arlen's back was completely to Ben now, as if Ben had ceased to matter.

"Have you lost your mind, rag doll?"

"Try me."

Arlen crept close to her.

She was so concentrated with adrenaline that she knew she wouldn't even feel his first, painful test of her true resolve.

Both of them knew that the longer she could last, the longer Jacob would be safe.

"I want her hand," Arlen said.

Willie obliged, leaving Ben quivering in his chair, his one, destroyed leg still untied. He wasn't going anywhere.

Going behind her, Willie loosened her ropes and allowed her one arm to go loose so she could extend it in front of her, offering it to Arlen as if he would kiss it.

He took it, delicately, like a gentleman, and raised it to his mouth full of sharp, filed teeth. Extending her pinky, he gripped her by the wrist, and slid the finger into the hot, watery opening of his lips. Then he bit down with all his might, right below her first knuckle.

24

THE CHALLENGE

Eleni kept a smile on her face, and it irritated Arlen. She had been right—her adrenaline was such that she could barely register this pain. She welcomed it, even; in the wake of so much terror, the pain was a kind of release, a focal point amid what had been so much hazy chaos. She smiled up at him through an almost imperceptible clenching of her jaw as his knife-like teeth worked against her pinky's delicate bone—and then she dug the nail of her pinky down into the fleshy cushion just beyond his lower teeth, stabbing him.

He noticed it, but it wasn't until she hooked the rest of her hand up to the side, turning her wrist around in his grip—willingly aiding him in the force of his bite by twisting her own flesh against his teeth—that his eyes widened slightly with surprise. Her thumb was out, arced gracefully, powerfully up—and it made square contact with his eye.

Her nail was filed, just as his teeth were. And she didn't hold back. Her only thought was to press in as deeply as she could, to keep driving and driving, and then to hook her thumb down, right inside the skull's border around the eye socket—and refuse to let him go.

His initial reaction was to struggle while still biting—but then, very quickly, he realized exactly how much harm she intended to do him. He dropped her pinky from his mouth and flailed, swatting her hand from his face like a dandy at a picnic who had been affronted by a bee. The release of her pinky only enabled her to reach out with her other fingers, digging her claws into his cheek, his entire face in her wretched grip. He hollered, and Willie wrapped his arms around Eleni's waist and chair, yanking her back. She didn't let go, not even when Willie began thudding the side of her face with his heavy fist. Arlen was dragged along with her, and the awkward mechanics of it all made Willie drop her, her chair clattering over on its side with her still securely in it.

Arlen's head was jerked down after her, and she knew she'd wrenched his neck in the process. The back of her chair broke in the fall. She heard it crack, even though it didn't come apart; she was still held in place. Arlen punched her in the face, but she just laughed at him and continued to laugh through the room going all black. It was pandemonium, all of them thrashing on the floor, but then she heard Mark shouting, "Stop, stop!" and saw his arm, no longer holding Jacob, looping around Arlen's waist to pull him back and restrain him. For a moment, she thought he was helping her, that he'd finally found his spine, but then she heard him say, "There's a car outside."

"In here, in here!" Eleni shrieked, loud and with glee, before Willie's heavy hand clapped over her laughing mouth. Mark finished prying her fingers from Arlen's face and her thumb from his eye socket. Her nose pushed hard breath against Willie's calloused hand, a hand which smelled like her chocolate-covered raisins, and she watched Arlen flounder back on the floor, pushing himself away from her by the heels of his feet.

He didn't cry or moan, but his shaky breath betrayed the fact that he, this demon creep, was seriously hurt and devastated at the realization of it. There was a pulpy disaster where his eye had been. Blood and goop cascaded from the newly emptied orifice, down over the nail-punctured flesh of his cheek. "Oh . . . oh . . ." he said as he gingerly touched a hand to his injuries, discovering the extent of them.

Eleni's pinky finger likewise gushed blood, and her thumb—the one that had been in Arlen's eye—looked like it had been dipped in red jelly. The flesh right below her pinky's first knuckle was a tattered fray. The bone, she realized only now, had absolutely been broken during the events of the last minute. It was all still connected, though, hanging on by whatever stretch of gristle she couldn't quite see beneath the thick coat of scarlet blood.

"Kill her," Arlen said, his voice completely different from how it had been up to that point, higher-pitched and fractured. "Kill all of them, this whole pathetic little family. But only after poking her eyes out. Only after she's seen you kill the kid."

"Shut *up*," Mark hissed, wrenching Arlen in his grip ever-so-slightly. "There's a cop out there."

Eleni craned her eyes to look toward the window over the bed, hot breath still puffing from her nose against Willie's meaty palm. Light from a car's headlights streamed in, brightening the room.

"Get her in the other room," Mark said, and Willie dragged Eleni, chair and all, back into the kitchen, around the wall, and out of sight. "Keep her quiet. Fuck."

As Eleni was pulled from view, she looked back to see Mark yanking the quilt from the bed and throwing it over the floor to cover up the bloodstains there. She furiously scanned the room for Jacob and saw him curled in a corner opposite from where the wolf had gone, hiding his face.

Arlen hobbled on his knees after her and Willie, to hide. Mark dragged Ben, also still in his chair, back with them too.

In the shadows of the kitchen, Eleni saw Mark stuff a rag into Ben's mouth and cover it over with duct tape. Mark looked frenzied, petrified. Ben wasn't even fighting, although what he'd witnessed had certainly helped pull him from his own pain and back into the present moment. Behind Ben, in his tied hands, Eleni saw a quick flash of something metallic . . . a small, rose-gold razor blade he had worked up out of his back pocket. Thin and singular, it would have been imperceptible to Willie's quick pat-down, completely un-feelable beneath the thick denim of Ben's jeans. Ben's bound hands aligned perfectly with that back pocket, his trembling fingers able to slip inside. He didn't look up or over at her at all. At a quick glance, he looked like he was lolling in his chair, but now Eleni knew his fingers were working.

Mark ran to the other room, and when he returned, his arms were full of the men's jackets, which he stuffed in a corner.

"Get the kid," Arlen hissed, and Mark ran back to the other room. Moments later, he returned with Jacob, who was sucking his thumb.

"Keep him quiet, Mommy," Mark said, dumping Jacob in her lap. Her one arm was still loose from its ropes, and Willie, as if giving an order, said, "She won't try anything, not with her kid right there in her lap." Her eyes bore holes into his as she kept up the same taunting, chilling air of control, but she simply looped her one free arm over Jacob and cradled him to her, smelling his hair.

"It's ok, baby," she whispered.

Willie pointed a gun to her temple and said, "Not a word."

25

THE ULTIMATUM

Even Jacob seemed to know to hold his breath in silence, as if he'd caught on to how things were going to work. Eleni felt his body fight for stillness as it curled tight to hers. Mark went to the front door. Eleni kept her eyes fixed on a rectangle of light on the floor, coming from the living room.

The officer rapped the door just a few times, and Mark opened it.

"Hey," Mark said breezily. She heard the tension in his voice even if the officer couldn't. "What brings you out here?"

The cop exhaled as if surprised, shaking his head. "Not you, that's for sure. Mind if I come in? Wolves are out."

Mark stepped aside, and Eleni heard the shutting of the door only feet away from where they were hiding. She began to draw in her last breath, fully expecting to shout for rescue and be killed. It didn't matter so long as Jacob was saved. But Willie, as if reading her mind, quickly moved the gun from her temple and jammed it into Jacob's back. Jacob sat up straighter, pushing against it, unsure of what it was. He looked at Eleni quizzically, and like a cartoon, Eleni felt her mouth snap shut.

"What the hell are you doing here, Byrnes?" she heard the cop ask, friendly. He knew Mark from town, where almost everyone knew everyone else. From the tone of his voice, she could tell the cop felt safe.

"I asked you first." Mark chuckled.

"Someone in town called in, saying they saw someone driving out to Ben's cabin," the cop said. So, someone had seen them . . . either Chaz's truck when he'd transported Eleni or this grisly trio . . . someone had been wanting to call in a hot tip on Ben Wilton, after all. "Not much goes on here. Everyone's been hot on that story for ages, as you know."

"Welp . . . just me."

"But how'd you get a key?"

"Ben gave me his spare a long time ago."

"But, Mark . . . you know, it's trespassing."

Eleni felt a flicker of hope as she heard something pivot ever-so-slightly in the cop's voice. Friend or no friend, perhaps he knew something was up.

She raised her eyes from the rectangle of light, only to find Arlen staring directly at her, not two feet away. His mangled face, his direct stare—the effect of it was ghastly in the dim light, like a gory Halloween mask come to hideous, breathing life. There was such intensity burning in his one remaining eye, his wide nostrils flaring as he fought his furious breath, that the strange but wonderful power trip she'd taken began to seep from her system, pushed by a pulsing, creeping cold that began on her spine and soaked outward, into one cell and then another.

"Oh, well . . ." Mark floundered a bit, then found himself. "You know it's kind of Eleni's now. Since they were living together . . ."

"Yeah."

"All his stuff. Not that we know he's dead or anything, but still . . . she has a right . . ."

"Still doesn't explain what you're doing here."

"Well, she and I, I mean . . ." Eleni heard Mark trail off into an awkward laugh. She could clearly picture the shrug, or the crude sexual fist-pump, indicating to the officer that they were now a thing.

"No kidding. You and Eleni? Ben's ex?"

"We never lost touch."

There was a slight pause.

"I'm gonna have to hear this from Eleni, though, Mark," the cop said. "I can't leave you here in her place without knowing she gave her say-so."

"C'mon, Pete. You know me."

"Don't make me keep asking."

Mark wavered again, then made another attempt.

"Well . . . she's here, actually. She's just asleep in the back."

"I'll wait right here."

"Well, she's had a rough night, you know."

"I'm sure she'll appreciate that I took the precaution."

"It's just, when you see her . . . I mean, don't get the wrong idea. She . . . she looks worse for wear."

"Why's that?"

It only took Mark a moment to land on his answer.

"She had a run-in with a wolf earlier tonight."

The cop sucked air through his teeth. Arlen, still holding Eleni with his eyes, smiled a red smile, his face becoming even more grotesque as Eleni fixated on him. That was her blood on his sharp teeth, only partially sucked away and swallowed.

"Oh, man, really? Why didn't you go back to town, get some help?"

Her blood, still lining every filed point, every crack in his dry lips.

"Well, nothing too serious. But we found a den of 'em in the basement. One almost took her finger off. She fell, hit her face in the fight. Lots of bumps and bruises, but it ran off when I fired a shot. They all did."

"Damn, she's lucky you were here."

"So, she's been down for the count awhile now. She didn't want to try to make it out to the truck, risk another attack. They can smell blood."

"Well, hell! Just let me talk to her for two minutes, and she can get back to resting."

"Ok. Give us a few minutes, ok?"

"Sure. Hey, mind if I use the facilities?"

"Be my guest."

The heavy footfalls of the cop crossed the room, and Eleni heard the close of the thin wooden door to the bathroom. The black, iron sliding lock slid into place. Mark rushed into the kitchen, scanned the room, and went straight to a roll of paper towels sitting on the counter.

"Fuck, we gotta get her cleaned up," he hissed, hurling a few paper towels into Eleni's lap, then turning to the sink. He pumped two waves of brackish water over another fistful of paper towels. "Wrap that around your finger," he commanded Eleni, looking over his shoulder.

It took Eleni a long, slow blink to break eye contact with Arlen. She didn't want to be the first to look away. Right as she turned her head to acknowledge Mark, she felt Willie's elbow roughly jab her in her side.

"Do what he says," he barked low, keeping the gun on Jacob. He jerked the ropes off her one still-bound arm so she could complete the task.

Eleni wound the paper towels into a tight, long strip, keeping her ravaged pinky finger extended out and away as her hands worked. Mark was quickly in front of her, mopping her face roughly with the dripping paper towels. She felt sharp stabs of pain as his hands passed over fresh bruises. "Hell, you have any makeup?" he asked her.

"No time for that," Arlen said, and his mouth bubbled slightly with blood when he spoke. "We've got sixty seconds, tops."

Mark smoothed her hair back, and comically, Arlen produced the elastic band he'd ripped out of her disheveled ponytail earlier so Mark could resecure it. He tried to position her hair to hide where she'd been hit with the log. Eleni looked to Arlen and waited. She knew there were orders coming, and he didn't disappoint.

"You tell him everything's all right and get him out of here," he said.

Mark grabbed some dry paper towels to wipe the water from her face. She tasted blood as a small trickle of water from her scrubbed face made its way between her lips.

"I've got nothing to lose by giving you up," she said, calm, tired. "We're dead anyway."

"You are," Arlen agreed. The jovial, confusing uncle from earlier was gone. In his place was a patient executioner. "You and your boy. But when it comes to Jacob, you know . . . we don't have to make it hurt. Not if you cooperate."

She looked down at Jacob huddled in her lap. Heard the small, "No say," his face pointed down and hidden.

"We don't have to make it hurt for your boy, but we will," he said, "if you don't do a good job."

Eleni glared at him. He always had one up on her, just as any abuser always had one up on a battered mother. They always knew she'd do whatever was necessary to protect the kid. There was no limit to it.

She heard the faint gust of the toilet as it flushed. The cop would be back soon.

"Besides, you know that even if you told that cop we're here, he'd never get out of here alive, don't you? Never radio in? He'd be shot through the head before he even understood what you said."

"They'd come looking for him," Eleni said.

"Who? The one other cop in town? Yeah, maybe. Tomorrow."

When Arlen blinked, only his good eye blinked. The eyelid over the other, ruined one simply hung lopsided, looking like rotten meat.

"By tomorrow, Eleni, you and your little boy will be a hundred miles from here, half-chewed by wild animals and ice-cold. Fuck. By the time they find you, you'll be so nibbled on they won't even be able to make a positive identification."

The bathroom door was opening. The ropes around her ankles were cut away.

"You want to be responsible for this guy's death too?"

The sound of the cop's boot-falls, walking across the room.

"So," Arlen continued, "go on. Be a good girl. Like you know how."

26

THE SMOKESCREEN

If there was one thing Eleni knew, it was, indeed, how to be a good girl. Her entire life, she'd always done whatever was asked of her. She'd always done things she didn't really want to, in the hopes of being treated right. The logic was that if she did all those things, she'd earn the basic, humane treatment everyone was supposed to get. Thing was, people like Arlen—and yes, Ben—didn't care to give that kind of treatment. They just wanted bowing and scraping.

Eleni stood, her thoughts feverish. Willie took Jacob and held a finger to his lips, momentarily becoming a nanny playing a game of silence. Mark lightly touched her elbow, as if to guide her, but she yanked her arm away and stepped into the rectangle of light being cast through the entryway to the main living area. He kept just a step behind.

She wished she could go back and relive her life. She wouldn't give even two seconds of her time to anyone who expected her to bow and scrape. Not even one second. In the end, she realized, when you allowed yourself to be taken advantage of, you opened doors for someone else to be hurt as well. The girlfriend in the next relationship, the child . . . the abuser walked through you and moved on to the next link in a chain that got uglier and uglier as it was allowed to grow. It would keep growing until someone, something, demanded they stop.

Raising her eyes, she saw an officer she'd seen before. It wasn't the one who had interviewed her and Ben; it was the other one. It took her a moment to land on the name—Officer Logan—and in the long second until it came to her, she just stared at him, standing near the foot of the disheveled bed. Didn't he wonder why she was sleeping in the other room when the bed was here?

Logan whistled, shrill, through his teeth.

"Oh, hell, girl, just look at you. You've been through it tonight."

She gave him a weak half-smile.

"It's been so long since I was here. I forgot to always be on the lookout."

She impressed herself by how friendly her voice sounded. This had always been a talent of hers, one she could never profit from but only be harmed by. She could always make things sound fine, even when they weren't.

"How'd it happen?"

"Well," she said, sighing. "I went down into the basement to check on the generator, and turns out, the cellar doors had been left open. For the past . . . three-and-a-half years, I guess."

Logan pulled a compassionate face at the mention of three-and-a-half years ago. It was a shared memory from two very different viewpoints.

"There's a den down there. Some brand-new wolf pups," she said.

"Now that it's March, they're all over."

"Well, I surprised 'em." She held up her hand, wrapped in paper towels. The towels were soaked-through pink, deepening to scarlet over the deepest part of her wound.

Logan whistled again.

"Real ugly sonofabitch too," she said, hoping Arlen would hear her, however childish it was. "With a messed-up face. Like something got *him* at some point."

"I'll be on the lookout—put him down if I see him," Logan said.

"You let me know if you get him."

"Jeez, I'm sorry that happened," he said. "Looks like you're bleeding an awful lot. I got a first aid kit in my truck. I could stitch you up? Everyone should have one around here."

"You know, I think there's one under the bathroom sink," she said, remembering.

"May I?" he asked, already moving toward it. She nodded.

In a flash, he was in and out of the bathroom, opening and closing the cabinet. He trotted back into the room with the kit under his arm, wearing the proud expression of a rescuer, and sat on the bed, patting the spot next to him. Ben's coat was right behind him, still where Arlen had thrown it. They had forgotten to stash it away with the rest of their coats. Eleni glanced at Mark, who had tension written all over his face, but she went and sat down.

"I've had to stitch up more drunks cut up in bar fights than you can imagine," Logan said, flipping open the lid on the first aid kit and rifling through the supplies. "Lots of broken bottles, faces full of glass."

He pulled on some latex gloves and took Eleni's hand, casting a glance up at Mark.

"You should've thought of this, Romeo. You let your girl go to bed all cut up?"

"I . . . I didn't think there was anything here."

"You gotta take care of each other out here." Logan winked at Eleni, who smiled at him. When she smiled, she felt the bruises along her jawbone under the tightening skin. Logan studied her for a minute. "Maybe I should take you back into town, see if we can't get the nurse?"

Eleni thought for a moment. She could say yes, say let me just get my son sleeping in the other room . . . but then would they kill Jacob, just like that, the moment they heard her say it?

"No," she said. "This is fine. This'll do."

Logan unwound the paper towels from her pinky, whistling yet again. It was as if the only response to seeing a severe injury was a whistle; regular words just wouldn't cut it. With each round of unrolling, the paper towels became more fully red, dripping, and ghastly. Finally, they were off, and there was the finger, mangled gristle and flesh hanging off her bone.

"Think I can see the bone right there," Logan said, gently lifting the hand by the wrist to get a better look. "Not sure how well I can patch this up, but I'll sure try."

It wasn't one slight cut. Putting Eleni's finger back together would be like working a quilt, trying to force the ragged pieces to fit.

Logan pulled out a sterilized needle and thread for stitching.

"Not the worst I've seen, though. Some of these animal attacks, the flesh is stripped right down to the bone."

He pulled out a small spray can of compressed numbing agent and, first giving a warning look to make sure she was ready, sprayed it liberally over the wound. Although the pain was nothing compared to what she'd already taken, she sucked air through her teeth. She was playing a part, after all.

"You'll still feel the pinprick, but hopefully, that'll help."

She kept her hand out obediently, and after carefully surveying the finger, Logan chose the spot to insert the needle. It went in smoothly, lubricated by all the blood, and he pulled it out the other side, dragging the long, coarse thread behind it. There was a dull pain in the center of the tugging sensation.

He worked carefully and quickly. At one point, she joked, "Gee, you have done this a lot," and he smiled. There was a genuine sweetness about him as he bent over her injury, repairing her.

176

Mark stood in front of them with his arms crossed. His desperation to have Logan leave was palpable. Eleni thought Logan picked up on it, too, and maybe went slightly slower because of it.

"So, how have you been?" Logan finally asked, not looking at her when he asked it. "This your first time back?"

She nodded.

"You gonna keep the cabin?"

She shrugged and made a show of looking around. That felt right for the part.

"I don't know. Might be too many painful memories."

Logan nodded, still gentle.

"Maybe Mark here will know someone in town who'll want to buy it," Eleni said, somewhat cheeky, smiling at Mark.

"So, when did you two . . . you know . . . ?"

Eleni shrugged. "We just stayed close through everything. It's really only been since we were in touch about what to do with the cabin."

"I was real sorry, thinking about everything you must've gone through," Logan said, meeting her eyes briefly, then getting back to work. "Heard you had a little one too."

"Yes, Jacob," she said.

"You're a brave woman," he said, and he gave her undamaged fingers a slight squeeze to punctuate this sentiment. No one had ever called her that before. She'd watched things online, videos designed to pump up the self-esteem of single mothers, that would use the word "brave." But this wasn't a word she'd heard from the actual people in her life. When they found out she was pregnant, the descriptors she'd heard from her own parents had been more along the lines of "idiot," "fool," "dummy," and "slut."

They hadn't come to the hospital when her son was born, and any encounters she'd had with them since had been fleeting. On several occasions, they'd asked her to come down to the small parking lot next to her apartment building so they could hand off some mail that had come to their house addressed for her, usually only passing it through their car window. They sent emails at odd intervals throughout the year, updating her on their health and complaining about their taxes. Then there was the day her mother ran into her at a supermarket and made awkward chitchat over the produce as Jacob, unacknowledged, kicked his legs against the grocery cart.

That had been the day before she got Chaz's message and accepted Ben's invitation.

"Think that's as good as I'm getting it," Logan said. Eleni examined the finger, still stained red from blood that had been wiped away. It was now a patchwork of tender bits of flesh, crisscrossed with sinister-looking, black, spiky knots. "Save you some blood, at least."

"Good thing I'm not a hand model," Eleni said, and Logan laughed politely. He carried the bloody paper towels and the needle into the bathroom, chucking the towels in the trash and rinsing off the needle. She heard the latex gloves snap off. The first aid kit remained open on the bed.

"Well," he said when he came back out, "guess I'll be on my way then. If you're sure you're all right?"

He looked between her and Mark, who had stayed standing, resolute, blocking the entryway to the kitchen throughout this entire process. It seemed as if Logan didn't believe she was all right, not even for a second. Mark said, "Oh, we're good," but Logan waited for Eleni to give her answer. She thought of that day when she gave her statement and how when her voice failed her, Ben stepped in to give her account. Kent had accepted Ben's voice as her own.

She thought about telling him, fast. But she knew he'd be dead in an instant and that it wouldn't save her child anyway.

"We're good," she echoed as she stood up. "Thanks so much for everything."

She walked with him the few steps to the door. Right before he opened it, she said, "They're still around. The wolves.

They're all over. Maybe . . . I mean, it might not be a bad idea if you just kept a lookout?"

"I will," he said, not quite getting it, "especially for that one with the injured face, like you said."

"They can really sneak up on you, so maybe even if you just, from your truck even, pulled around and checked around the cellar doors or something . . ."

She searched for a code. Something she could say to get him to stay while at the same time not alerting the other men who listened, invisible.

"Tell you what. I'll drive around, do a sweep, and maybe stop back later on just to be sure?"

She nodded, a lump forming in her throat.

"That'd be great. Thank you."

Mark scoffed, shook his head. "She's all shook up, but nothing's getting in here."

Nothing's getting out either.

Logan was pulling his gun from its holster, and for a moment, Eleni thought he'd noticed everything and that he was getting the jump on her tormentors.

But then, she realized, he was simply pulling it out to keep it at the ready as he got to his car.

"Thank you," she said. "That was really nice of you."

"You rest up now. Feel better," he said, nodding at her before opening the door.

"Please stay safe."

He vanished out into the cold, dark morning. Through the window, Eleni watched as he got in his car, drove once around the house, and headed back into the woods.

She didn't know if he was looking at her from inside the car or how clearly he could see her. Clenching her hands in front of her, she got close to the window. She contorted her face into a panicked, urgent expression and frantically gestured with her fingers toward herself, hoping he would realize she was trying to tell him something. Her little gesture was silent and hidden from the room behind her and her best chance.

But soon, his red tail lights vanished beyond the cover of the pines.

She heard Arlen's footfalls as he came back up behind her and felt the gun in her back.

"Now," he breathed in her ear, in control again, "let's get back to our fun."

27

THE SURPRISE

"Thank you so much for your help, Mommy," Arlen said, mocking her.

Eleni backed away from the window, gently pulled by his hand, the gun stuck stubbornly between her shoulder blades.

"Mark," Arlen snapped, "go out and down the path a ways. Make sure that asshole is really gone."

Mark, dutiful again, went for the door, holding his own gun up at the ready. He'd shoot any wolves he saw as target practice if nothing else. Willie shut and locked the door behind him.

"Mommy here got a little cute," Arlen said, shoving Eleni forward once she was again facing the room. Willie brought her broken chair back into the room in case Arlen wanted to use it. Then he dragged Ben, in his chair, back to where the action was, leaving him right at the entryway to the kitchen. Ben looked more alert now, eyes sharp above his shattered knee. The knee splitter was still on him, winched tight.

Jacob toddled out from the kitchen, following them. He was scared, but Eleni knew he'd be more scared left alone in the other room in the dark. For a moment, he looked like he would run to Eleni, but she held up her hand in a small, stop gesture, and his feet padded to a halt right inside the living area.

181

"No more games," Arlen said. "I do enjoy them, but you play dirty."

That doesn't hurt my feelings. Is that supposed to hurt my feelings?

I'm sick of all the dirtiest cheats in the world always saying everyone else is a cheat.

"Simple execution style's the way to go. Your whole miserable little family—"

"You said you'd let the baby go," Eleni said, even though she knew he'd said nothing of the kind.

Ben used to always say she'd said things she hadn't. It had worked on her a lot of the time, making her second-guess herself. It was a last-ditch effort.

"So, that's your best hope now?" Arlen sneered. "That the shit-for-brains cop will come back and find your toddler sitting next to your dead bodies? That's your best possible outcome?"

Eleni stayed quiet.

"You're all dying. Your best possible outcome is if I do it quick."

Eleni stood in the center of the room now. Arlen circled her like the animal he was. She slowly turned, trying to keep eyes on him. Under this guise of just trying to keep pace, she came up close to her chair. Willie had placed it near to the small wooden table.

The ropes were gone, stashed somewhere.

Arlen cocked the gun, aimed directly at her face.

Eleni grabbed the chair and threw it.

It missed Arlen, sailing a good two feet to the right.

He laughed.

He laughed, but it wasn't him she'd been trying to hit.

If she'd hit him, it would have done nothing. A split second, and he would have knocked the chair away.

No. She'd thrown it squarely at the corner table, the one draped over with a red tablecloth.

She threw it squarely at the wolf mother she knew was still sitting there, licking her wounds.

She threw it, knowing that if that mother had an ounce of strength in her body, an ounce of animal instinct left, the room would soon be in chaos.

She was right.

The chair clattered to the floor right in front of the table, falling to its side and skittering into the tablecloth. Eleni, who knew to listen for it, heard the mad scrabble of claws, affronted, getting the mother on her feet. She heard the furious snap and snarl of a startled beast. The wolf surged out from under the tablecloth, blood soaking the fur at her throat, and Arlen didn't have time to react quickly enough. He was the closest to the wolf, and she was on him in an instant.

Arlen crumpled to the ground as she pounced. The surprised expression on his face didn't even have time to change into one of fear. He went from smug, to surprised, to howling as the wolf mother's teeth tore into him. The flesh of his forearm was reduced to bloody ribbons as he held it up over his face, trying to hold her off. Her frenzied yelping and growling made a hysterical, other-worldly cacophony. Willie came forward, aiming his gun, but he couldn't get a clear shot in the helter-skelter battle going on.

Eleni ran and picked up Jacob, snuggling him to her.

Willie fired, somehow missing both man and beast.

The wolf raised her head, her mouth full of a portion of Arlen's throat, and lunged at Willie.

He folded under the impact of her weight, as Arlen had done, but wasn't able to hold her off nearly as long. She sank her teeth into his tender neck and, thrashing and screaming, firing once more, Willie's life was violently ripped from his body.

But his last shot ripped through the wolf's ribcage, taking her life as well.

The wolf jerked sideways up into the air, her muzzle slamming with a crack against the wooden tabletop as she dropped to the ground, dead.

Eleni watched, pressing Jacob's face protectively into her chest.

She heard Mark outside, running back toward the door at the sound of the commotion.

You never run in front of predators. You never run. Then they know you're prey.

This was a fact Mark remembered too late. His calls of "what's going on?" suddenly switched into a panicked "open up, let me in!" His fists pounded on the wooden door that Willie had locked as a safety precaution only minutes earlier. The door rattled in its frame, and Eleni heard snarling and barking. Along with Mark's fists, there was the sound of claws on wood, apex predators bounding up the porch steps. Their bodies occasionally thudded into the door as they attacked Mark. He screamed, shrill and desperate, amidst the sound of a feeding frenzy. He fired shots, but there were too many. Mark's screams were soon gone, but the ripping and snapping sounds remained for minutes after as the wolves enjoyed their meal.

Eleni hugged Jacob close.

"Mommy. Mommy, it's so bad."

"I know. We're gonna get out of here, baby. We're getting out of here."

The sun would be up soon. She'd have a window of light to make things a little easier. After finding Arlen's keys, she'd take a gun out to the car to shoot off any animal that came close. She'd get back through the woods, somehow steering her way through. Or Logan would come back and find her before then. They were getting out of here.

And in the meantime, she wouldn't let Jacob see any more of this.

She walked to the bed, Jacob's face firmly buried against her, and pulled off the sheet. Trembling, the shock and speed of it all hit her. Perhaps the most startling thing on earth was to see how quickly someone—even multiple someones—could be killed. The quilt, which had already been lain on the floor to hide blood, was now covered with bodies: two human, one canine. She draped the sheet over them as best she could. It was dark blue, so even though the blood would soak through, its frightening color wouldn't be immediately apparent to her child.

"Mommy, we go home," Jacob pleaded.

Then, right as she was about to let the sheet drop from her hand, Eleni heard a ragged breath.

She pulled the sheet back slightly.

Arlen was still alive.

28

THE ALPHA

Eleni looked down at Arlen, her head tilted to one side, like a benevolent painting of the Madonna. She was in awe of the fact that his breath was still wheezing along in its damaged windpipe, inside the tattered mess of his throat. She continued to gaze at him, holding up the corner of the sheet in one hand. Jacob straightened in her arms and looked back over her shoulder toward the kitchen.

"You'll be dead soon," she told Arlen, and there wasn't anything menacing in her voice. She didn't feel the need to taunt and torment him, as he would have done to her. It was a simple statement of a fact.

His breath whistled, his eye fastening on her face. Under the sheet lay the wolf's body where it had fallen over his shin. The wolf didn't struggle for breath; she was a heavy hulk of musty fur, and Eleni wondered if Arlen was still aware enough to sense that through his jeans.

His eye sparkled in the light of the fire that was, once again, growing dim.

"A bitch after all," he said, barely audible, and Eleni wasn't sure if he meant her or the wolf.

"Mommy," Jacob said, and his one hand tugged at her hair. Eleni, transfixed, didn't respond. She waited to see the various cords inside Arlen's throat rattle to their final close.

She kept watching him, marveling silently at the violent life now disappearing before her eyes.

He said, "It's worse for you. Gonna be worse for you." He looked crazy, but then again, he always had.

She asked the question he wanted her to ask, in spite of herself. "Why's that?" She didn't expect any kind of real answer, but there was a sort of hypnotism taking place.

"Cause I never believed he loved me," Arlen said.

Jacob kept shaking the fistful of hair he held. "Mommy," he insisted, "Daddy's up."

Daddy's up.

Eleni turned around slowly.

In the doorway to the kitchen stood Ben. He leaned heavily on the chair to which he'd previously been tied, using it as a crutch. The knee splitter was still in place, so deeply embedded in his leg it was essentially holding it together at this point. In his other hand, he held the thin, flat razor blade she had seen him working earlier.

He was gazing down at Arlen, too, but there was nothing benevolent in his face. No reverence for watching a life, however terrible, snuff out.

Somehow, he seemed taller than Eleni had remembered, despite his injuries. He was hulking, hunched forward, expression threatening. The red and yellow interplay of bruises and blood that streaked across his face turned it into some terrifying, painted war mask. The whites of his eyes stood in stark contrast to his battered skin, giving them an eerie, other-worldly quality. He was like an angel of death or a devil come to collect Arlen's soul.

He moved toward the wretched near-corpse that had been Arlen and which was now somewhere between that horrible person and a macabre death-mask himself. Ben hopped his good leg forward, dragging the chair along for balance. As he came nearer to Eleni, Ben seemed to tower even higher, and she could only imagine what he looked like to Arlen as he drew ever closer to his crushable skull, lying there on the floor.

When Ben was close enough that the bangs and scrapes of traversing the floor with the chair had quieted down, Arlen, in his fading voice, said:

"You're worse than me. Pretender."

Ben kept looking down, tilting his head slightly at the mash-up of flesh speaking to him.

"Eleni thought you were good. I'm sure Aimee did too."

Ben smiled down at Arlen then. Eleni watched it, the way his mouth twisted, so brightly painted in blood and bruises. It was ghoulish.

"You know all that you did," Arlen said.

"And so do you," Ben said, speaking finally. "And you're the one that's gotta face it all, right now, when you have what? About thirty seconds to live?"

"I should've killed you when I had the chance," Arlen said, each word a forced, painful choke. Eleni remembered her own clichés earlier in the night. Arlen was at the point of clichés now.

Ben leaned over, looking at him even more closely.

"And I should've killed you the night I killed Aimee."

With that, Ben, perfectly balanced on his good leg, lifted the chair at his side and began to slam it up and down, into Arlen's face, pummeling over and over until Arlen was nothing more than a red burst, exploded across the floorboards.

Eleni pressed Jacob's face to her again, moving away from it all, toward the bathroom. She closed her eyes, too, despite everything she'd seen that night—closed them so she wouldn't actually see this Ben, this monster, doing this thing. She only opened her eyes again when the sound of the pummeling stopped.

When she looked, she saw that Ben, standing over Arlen's ruined body, was now looking straight at her.

29

THE PLEA

Eleni waited for a long moment, refusing to break eye contact with Ben. Neither one knew how to begin. Her eyes eventually traveled down to his destroyed knee, so much clotted meat gathered around the knee splitter . . . something in her told her to keep things light, even if only for a few moments. No hard questions. No devastating revelations. She needed to pretend as if, even standing over these dead bodies, nothing had changed.

"Do you want to take that off, or . . . ?" she asked, looking pointedly at the knee splitter. It sounded like a weird sexual invitation.

He glanced down, then back at her.

"I'm going to do a splint around it. It's one of those things that's worse if you take it off."

He had definitely seen it used on someone before, maybe seen it taken off after. Maybe their leg had simply ripped off, pulled by its own weight after that, when they tried to move.

"We have aspirin, although I don't know if it'll do any good," she said.

"You could probably use some of that yourself."

They looked at each other for a long time. Like an old married couple used to seeing each other out by the picket fence, now suddenly seeing each other covered in gore.

191

Ben moved toward her—one hop, then another—but stopped short of her and reached for his jacket, still on the bed. Beneath it, he found the orange bottle of prescription pills with no label. He poured what seemed a near-dangerous amount into his palm, then dry-swallowed them as Eleni looked away.

Eleni walked, staying casual, nothing of running prey in her motions. Leaving a wide berth as if she were just skirting the carnage on the floor, she passed Ben and went to the table, where all of Jacob's medical supplies were spread out, left messy after his last attack. Still holding Jacob, who was now twisting around to look at his father, she started to pack it all into the bag.

She needed it ready so she could grab it and take it with her. When she ran.

But now, it was all casual, a mother simply tidying the nest.

Her eyes landed on a long, sharp wolf's tooth lying on the table. It must have cracked right out of the wolf mother's mouth when she was flung back by Willie's bullet, slamming her muzzle against the wood. Something in Eleni hurt when she saw it.

"That can wait, can't it?" Ben asked. He stooped to pull the sheet back up over Arlen's destroyed head.

Eleni grabbed the tooth and tucked it, along with the last of Jacob's supplies, into the bag. She looked at Ben again but not before noting how the keys to the seaplane were also splayed on the table right beside her.

After another long moment, he asked it.

"Are you still for me, Ells?"

"For you?"

"For me or against me?"

She swallowed. Amazingly, Jacob was beginning to drowse against her shoulder, although maybe it wasn't that amazing, given the tremendously traumatic events he'd just experienced. He was wiped out, exhausted. It reminded her of when he was only a few months old, and she'd taken him to a cousin's wedding. The loud music, the lights—it was unlike anything he'd seen or heard before. It was as if he'd lifted his head, took one look around the ballroom, and promptly passed out in her arms.

She put a protective hand on his back, although, to Ben, it just looked like a mother patting her sleeping baby.

Not a mother trying to block him from coming any closer.

"I'll always be for you," she said, and it was almost physically painful to say it.

Ben smiled and sighed, seeming to relax. She didn't think she imagined it—there was a tear in his eye.

"So, that's my boy there, then?"

She nodded, tears in her eyes too.

"Can I hold him?"

Ben took one half-hop forward. Eleni hesitated, pulling her breath in, going one step back.

Ben froze.

"Well," she said, Ben's face already falling into a scowl, "maybe get cleaned up first? You're pretty bloody. Don't want that to be his first memory of you, right?"

She chuckled nervously, realizing as she offered this feeble excuse that she was bloody too. Ben seemed to accept this, though, the scowl evaporating.

He hobbled to the fireplace and grabbed some of the longer boards that were there, leftovers from the construction of the cabin that had found their way into the woodpile and would do for a splint. He hopped to the bed, dropping them next to him with a clatter, and proceeded to pull off and rip up the fitted sheet still on the mattress. Exposing the mattress, showing all of its stains, almost felt like a violation. Despite the dust, it had begun the night looking so inviting, covered with a quilt on which they'd made love. Now, it was bare.

She watched quietly as he rigged boards on either side of his leg and tied them tight, fashioning an awkward boot to protect his injury. It didn't look to her like it was going to be a particularly comfortable solution.

"You have a high pain tolerance," she said.

He chuckled as he worked, sweat popping out on his brow. He glanced at her.

"So do you, by the look of it."

The doctor said that to her when she'd given birth. *High pain tolerance.* It was like a badge of honor. But she wondered, too, just how often in her life she'd refused to acknowledge pain until it was too far gone. There was agony in her life that probably never needed to be there.

When Ben finished crafting the wooden casing for his leg, he looked at her.

"I was hoping it'd be a different kind of reunion, but at least we'll be leaving together, which is more than I could've hoped for an hour ago."

"How?" she asked carefully. "That cop will be back, you know."

"I got the seaplane. Just down the trail. Once the sun's up, you can help me down. The three of us. Together."

Her mind whirled, reaching for different word combinations, different options that could help to undo what was happening.

"Where have you been? Where would we go?"

"I've been in and out of every shit, backwoods town in Alaska, along the coast," he said, waving an arm as if to encompass all those "towns" consisting of a few ramshackle cabins where rebels in the woods were lodged. "Some places without even any names. No technology to speak of. Surrounded by a thousand miles no human feet ever touched. I'd fly up and down, get grounded by the weather . . . winters were a bitch."

"Do you . . . I mean . . ." she trailed off. "Did you have the money Arlen was looking for?"

Ben laughed. "What, you after me for my money now?"

Answer the question. "Well, Arlen sure was."

She paused, then heard herself say it, even as she told herself not to say it.

"After that, and . . . after revenge. For . . ."

Say her name.

". . . Aimee."

Ben's eyes, gradually taking on a glassy quality since his palmful of pills, quickly focused. "I had nothing to do with what happened to that girl. I barely knew her. They'd lock me away forever, Ells, and it wasn't me. I'm about dead set it was Arlen himself. That's why you've gotta come with me. Give me something of a life, now that they took mine away. Give me a partner, a kid. Fuck, it's been so lonely."

As he spoke the word *lonely*, she knew he'd been sleeping with women in these various towns, picking people up and spending the night. Maybe that was how he got a roof over his head. For all she knew, he'd maybe had full relationships in these intervening years, months spent with this one, then that. He probably gave them fake names, fake stories to build up dramatic romances that eventually left the women in knots, blaming themselves for wrongs they'd never actually committed.

The fire popped and crackled.

"But you said to Arlen, right before you . . ." she trailed off. "You said, 'The night I killed Aimee.'"

She was being stupid, but that something in her, the something that had flared up with Arlen, stirred again.

"I didn't say that," he said, a dark look on his face.

However strong the feeling was, she needed to be smart. She could spend the rest of her life telling and demanding the truth—however long it might be, if she could get out of here. But right now, she had a plan and just needed to stick to it.

"Oh," she said.

"You must've misheard me. Not really surprising, what with all the trauma tonight."

"Oh. Ok."

*But I saw her picture. I saw it up there behind the stones.
Buried.*

"You believe that, right?" he asked, studying her face
carefully.

She nodded, maybe too quickly, then tried to nod slowly.
Maybe too slowly.

He only observed her.

"I still love you," he said, and she believed him when he
said it.

The problem was just that he didn't actually know how to
love her or anyone. That part of him was broken.

"I still love you too," she said, and she believed that too.
She did love him, based simply on what had passed between
them. Based on knowing he was broken. But . . .

She nodded toward the bathroom door. "Go clean up?
Then hold the baby?"

The fire popped again. It was dying. She looked at it, then
looked to Ben for permission. Once he nodded, she went to
the fire and threw another log on, followed by more kindling.

There was one smooth board in the woodpile that could
wedge just perfectly through the door handle of the bathroom.
The door opened in, so if she slid it through there, it would
lock Ben in, even if only for a few moments. With the time
bought by his bad leg and the fact that he might not be able
to break through quickly, she could grab Jacob's bag, grab the
keys to the seaplane, and either yank up the sheets to find
Willie's gun or grab a knife in the kitchen before running out
through the basement.

She was now standing right beside the board, waiting.

"I'm so tired," Ben said. "Just so tired of all of it."

She stayed mute.

He pushed himself up from the bed, balancing carefully
on the splint he'd concocted. It was clear he couldn't put
much weight on it, that each step was excruciating, but he

didn't need to use the chair as a crutch as he hobbled over to the bathroom door.

She took a tentative step closer to the board, waiting for him to go in.

"You gonna do a full shower?"

"Top half only," he said, arriving at the doorway and resting against it. "I'll swab around the knee."

Just another few steps . . . perhaps she'd even trail him in, being helpful, then shove him down. He'd flounder getting back on his feet. She'd jam the board in, grab the bag, the keys . . . maybe the hand axe from the fireplace. They would make it. She and Jacob would make it.

Ben looked at her from the bathroom doorway with a sad look on his face and shook his head.

"Oh, Ells," he said, then pivoted away from the bathroom, taking a hop-step in her direction.

She took an instinctive half-step back.

Ben pulled out the switchblade he must've picked back up once he'd gotten free, when she hadn't been looking at him. It clicked open with a *schk!* and glistened in the fire glow.

"Don't you know who you're dealing with?"

30

THE COMMITMENT

Within minutes, Ben forced Eleni back into one of the wooden chairs to be tied in place when he went to shower.

In the chair. Again.

"Please," she said, not asking to go free. "Just let me keep his medicine bag on my lap. In case he has an attack, and you're not here."

"How do I know he's mine? Really mine?" Ben asked, eyes boring holes into her own.

She didn't break eye contact.

"I haven't even been with anyone else since you were gone."

It was the truth, and she knew he would love it. It had only been the two of them that whole summer, here in this cabin, when she got pregnant. It was impossible for Jacob to be anyone else's. She'd been unable to go out on her own, and no one ever came here unless it was one of Ben's friends, to see him. Come to think of it, she was pretty sure he'd never even left her alone in a room with *them*—at least, not for any longer than it would have taken him to run to the bathroom or go to the kitchen for another beer. He hadn't trusted her for as much as ten minutes, and he hadn't trusted his friends either.

If his mistrust ran so deep that he expected immediate betrayals the moment his back was turned, what did it say about the kind of things he himself contemplated doing to others?

Ben dropped the medicine bag in her lap and proceeded to tie her to the chair. It had become so commonplace, getting tied to this chair, that she almost laughed through her fear. Jacob slept deeply on her lap, once again crisscrossed with rope. Her right hand rested on the zipper of the bag. Ben proceeded to tie her arm tight across the wrist, but she had just enough motion with the hand to fumble medicine from the bag if need be.

When Ben was done, dripping sweat from both pain and exertion, he slumped onto the bed, staring at her. After a while, he gazed at Jacob, and she saw affection in his eyes.

"He does look like me."

"I know," she said. "I think of you every time I look at him."

And then, because it was the truth and because she was most likely going to die very soon in her spent, ruined, wrung-out body, she said, "I loved you so much, you know."

Tears dripped down onto the ropes that were lashed over her chest and child.

"Were you loyal?"

"I was."

"You know everything now, though, don't you? Do you still love me, knowing everything?"

"About Aimee?"

"You know," he said, "it was never real love if you don't still love me now."

"Can't love change? Be different?"

"There's only one kind."

The fire crackled. She waited, watching the light from the flames pull at the shadows on his face.

"And what kind is that—to you?" she asked. It was the most authentic conversation they'd actually ever had about love, about each other. "What exactly do you think love is, Ben?"

"Unwavering," he said, staring directly at her, eyes fixed as if to punctuate the word. It was something that would sound romantic to a girl sitting across from a handsome guy on a date. *Unwavering love.* The implications of it would go undetected. She wouldn't realize until much later she'd been saddled with a responsibility to withstand all sorts of torture. "Unwavering."

"No matter what someone does to you?"

"And what did I ever do to you, besides love you?"

Her throat felt so tight it hurt. "They could have killed me. Killed Jacob. They almost did. They were still going to—"

"But you were pretty clever, weren't you? A few tricks up your sleeve. I always knew you couldn't be as innocent as you pretended."

"It was our last chance."

"'Our'—yours and his," Ben scoffed, nodding at Jacob. "You would've left me here. Left me behind."

"I wouldn't have killed you."

"You would've gone and turned me in."

She hesitated; she hadn't actually thought about that, although she supposed, now, that she certainly would have as soon as she was safely away.

"Smarter people than you have tried to catch me," he said. "They never did, and you won't either."

Her mind and voice were both stalled out, trapped around an idea she was trying to express. It was the same one that she'd always tried so hard to understand when she was with him and never actually could.

"If you think love's unwavering, and you think you love me," she finally managed, "then why are you turning on me?"

"The love hasn't changed. But I gotta react to what you're doing."

"Can't I react too?"

"Your reaction is to turn into a traitor."

"I never betrayed you. I fought for you up until tonight."

"So, you admit it. Now you've turned on me."

"I just don't . . . want . . . this."

He took a ragged breath through his nose and let out a long exhale.

"But you said you were mine. You promised it."

"You promised me a lot of things too."

"Nothing I didn't stick to."

"You promised me . . . you swore to me . . . that you didn't kill her."

"It was no business of yours if I did."

"It was."

"Our love was separate from all that."

More hot, fat tears dripped from her cheeks. "I wanted to keep it pure too. But it's just not reality."

"You're an expert on reality now?"

"On my own, I guess."

"You've got everything all wrong," he said, his insistence coming back. Forceful. "You don't understand what happened, and you never will. And you're throwing everything away."

"I just . . . want . . . to go."

A beat.

"Well, you're not going. If I decide to take you with me tonight, you'll come with me."

"And if you don't?"

"I can't trust you alive."

"I did nothing to you, Ben."

"Nothing? You'd have me rot in jail. You'd throw me in there. The father of your child."

"You killed someone."

He leaned forward from the edge of the bed, close to her face.

"I did kill her," he said, his eyes wild. "I killed her in the most brutal way I could think of. And they didn't catch me. And she wasn't the only one. I've killed ones I don't even think they know about. Sluts nobody misses. I'm good at it;

I enjoy it. And they didn't catch me, Eleni. And if I choose to kill you and leave you here tonight? They aren't going to catch me for that either."

She only stared at him. There was nothing left to say. It was foolish to even try. He was a labyrinth that sealed up behind you once you were in. There was no way to solve it.

He came one inch closer.

"So, if I were you, I'd hope that I choose to bring you with me. To give you another chance, although God knows, you don't deserve it after all you've done. A chance to start over with me. I'm not giving you up. So, it's one way or another. You come with me, or . . . you don't. You die here. But either way, you're mine until you stop breathing. There's a promise for you."

Staring into her eyes, he began to rise, leaning over, balancing as much as he could on his good leg.

He kissed her, his lips salty from both sweat and blood, then stood up fully. His taste lingered on her.

Tenderness washed over his face, then he laughed.

"Lucky you didn't bite me. You look feral."

He hop-clomped over to the bathroom.

"I'm cleaning up," he said. "Don't move an inch, not that you even can. Just sit here and think. While I decide what to do with you."

31

THE TEETH

Ben left the door to the bathroom wide open when he went in to clean off. "I'll be able to hear everything," he told her before disappearing into the glare of bright fluorescent lights from over the bathroom sink, a contrast to the natural, orangey glow of the light in the living room. Eleni sat for what felt like a long time, waiting for the hiss of the shower water to come on. She thought about who she'd been when she thought Ben loved her. He had praised her submissiveness, put it on a pedestal, tricked her into making it something she wanted to preserve. She thought about how never sticking up for herself hadn't made her a "good girl." It had simply allowed bad people to do bad things to her.

If they ever got out of here, how would she talk to Jacob, how would she show him a different way of being "good" than the way she had adopted? The way that had led them to this moment right now? There had to be a different standard, a new code to live by; there was no bravery or strength in simply accepting bad treatment. Yes, there had been bravery and strength in the withstanding of torment, but to simply accept it and make no effort to change it? Was that what she wanted to show her kid? Is that who she wanted to be?

She thought of her mother then, the mother she tried not to think of—even though the not thinking of her sometimes felt like the greater acknowledgment. There was bravery when she stepped between Eleni and her father to divert attention, to give Eleni time to leave, and to receive a blow originally inspired by some of Eleni's childhood naughtiness. But when it came time to insist the hitting stop or when it came time to pack a bag and run, the bravery was absent. And the people in their lives—relatives, friends, Eleni's father—always seemed to applaud the fact that Eleni's mother withstood it and stayed.

All except one friend. The woman was having tea with Eleni's mother in the kitchen one day when Eleni overheard her say, "It takes courage to stay, but it takes more courage to leave." Eleni couldn't remember ever seeing that friend again. She was probably never welcome after that.

Eleni eventually packed her own bag. She'd thought it was for something better, but it wound up being for more of the same.

Her mind flashed on the idea of staying with Ben and trying to appease him. How long would she and Jacob survive if she did that? Would they get extra days, months, years? Would it be worth it to barter self-respect and autonomy for time?

Whatever filter had lain over her heart all these years had been turned off tonight. It was the filter that allowed others' words and actions to seep through while at the same time holding at bay the corresponding, proper emotional responses that would allow her to get mad or to leave them. Was there a strength in continuing to accept bad treatment? Maybe, on some level. But she no longer accepted it.

"It takes courage to stay, but it takes even more courage to leave."

She knew that the moment she got out of this chair, she'd likely be killed. It didn't matter.

She was ready to leave.

Her son, the only reason she might have stayed sitting, lay helpless in her arms, trusting her. She was an oasis in the midst of all he'd seen tonight, and she wondered, if he lived, exactly how much he'd remember.

If she stayed sitting, there was perhaps a better chance of his surviving. But to be what, to witness what, eventually? Because she was certain that if she stayed, sooner or later, she'd be killed.

If she got up, they were both in danger, but there was a small chance they would make it.

She heard a slight stirring coming from the kitchen. A faint shuddering of a loose board, followed by a gentle stepping over the lower half of the block table. Her breath caught as she waited for whatever it was to come into the living room.

At first, she thought it was another rat—it was so small. But as it came fully into the room, she could see it was a wolf pup.

She didn't know how to judge its age, but it was very young, younger than any she'd ever seen in the wild. That litter had been near to brand-new. The pads of the pup's paws were still pink, as were its nose and even its lips, and the ears were still flopped over. It made a pathetic mewling noise as it swayed in on small, stubby legs. She thought the men killed all the wolf pups. They said they had, but clearly, they'd missed at least this one.

Her eyes pricked with tears looking at it. Had this been the smart one or simply the lucky one? The one who knew to hide in some dark, frosty corner of the basement until the noise subsided? Even as young as this, it had followed its mother's scent up, through the hole in the door, over the minefield of the table-barrier, and into this room.

They hadn't killed it, but she knew it would die without its mother to protect it.

"I'm sorry," she whispered, watching its unsteady progress into the room, paw pads tentatively setting out onto the sheet that covered the bodies. It arrived at the lump that was its mother, some blood seeping through the cloth, sniffed at her, and whimpered.

Jacob would die without Eleni. If not literally, then in spirit. Could she imagine this child, this being still forming and vulnerable to the input all around him, hiding out in Alaskan back alleys, bunking on couches in one-room cabins while his "father" screwed the women he picked up? Or imagine him being acclimated to thoughts of killing as Ben justified it to him, over and over, as if his father was the only one living normally? Eleni herself had been brainwashed, and she'd come to Ben as an adult with alleged abilities to reason rationally. What would Jacob become? Assuming Ben didn't beat him to death before he grew up or that he didn't wind up in a home . . .

Beyond the bathroom doorway, Ben grunted as he worked his way out of his shirt. The shower water finally came on, but it wouldn't be a full shower. He'd keep the splinted leg out of the water, propped on the toilet as he sat on the edge of the tub, then lean his head and naked torso back to wash the blood away in a cascade of brackish well water. It wouldn't take long.

Her one free hand, swiveling on its pinned wrist, unzipped Jacob's medicine bag.

She dug in and felt around, straining against the rope that rubbed against an internal knot alongside her wrist bone. She was sure her body was full of knots, every cell contorted and bunched up like a scared cat.

She felt and felt, couldn't find it, and then . . .

It raked over her finger.

The wolf tooth.

She managed to work it up, grasped firmly between her thumb and forefinger, and pulled it out. Eyeing the tight, intricate knot lashed over her front, beside her pinned wrist and about halfway down Jacob's bicep, she angled the tooth, then began to pick at the tangled nest of rope. She dug it into the crevices, pushing it, working it, opening the crevices wider, making the knot incrementally looser and looser. The baby wolf licked at the lump under the sheet; whether it was out of affection or a need for milk, who knew.

It would need both if it wanted to live.

The pup pulled at the sheet with its small nubs of teeth. Eleni wiggled the large tooth in her fingers back and forth in a widening loop.

As the knot loosened marginally, Eleni worked even deeper with the tooth. She felt the knot giving, the intense pressure of the rope over her working wrist lessening, ever-so-slightly. The wrist gained greater movement. She tucked the tooth into her palm, holding it in place with her thumb in case she needed it again, and used her three good fingers to dig in, tug, and unravel.

The knot finally gave entirely. It was still wound in loops she had to un-wind, but its strength was zapped. Her fingers now moved unrestricted, wrist pulled free of the binds. She yanked and guided the rope off and away from Jacob, then set to work undoing the knots around her ankles. It was hard to bend while holding her son; she began to sweat, and her breathing grew labored, but after a few agonizing minutes, and with the help of the tooth, she was pulling her feet through the semi-tight openings she'd made. The damaged foot, still bearing wounds from the knee splitter, sang as it forced its way through.

She stood up.

Slinging the medicine bag over her shoulder, she hoisted Jacob up so his head could rest in the crook of her neck. The wolf tooth went into her front sweatshirt pocket, as did the keys to the seaplane. As silently as she could manage, she turned to the fireplace and took up the small hand axe.

She kept her eyes on the entry to the bathroom. The water continued steadily. There was nothing to indicate Ben had been alerted.

Axe at the ready, she lay Jacob on the bed and got their coats. She quickly outfitted the unconscious toddler before pulling on her own gear. A quick glance out the window showed two hulking, canine forms pacing the boards of the porch, still sniffing. A thin line of blood seeped under the front door into the living room, and she knew Mark lay right beyond that barrier, dead, partially consumed, and likely still reaching to pound for entry. There was no going that way. She lifted Jacob back up and turned to go but hesitated.

In spite of herself, she went instead to that stripped, laid-bare mattress and grabbed one of the pillows.

What are you doing?

She yanked the pillowcase off, leaving the pillow as exposed and unattractive as the mattress.

Is it that you don't really want to go? That you're scared to finally go?

She carefully picked her way over the dead bodies under the sheet, at one point accidentally stepping on the squishy hand of one of her tormentors, unable to avoid it.

The sheet over Arlen's ruined face was soaked through with blood. Two deep pools of dark red sat where his eyes would have been, giving the impression he was watching her as she passed over him.

She held the pillowcase with the same hand that supported Jacob's bottom. With her free arm outstretched, she bent and scooped up the wolf pup, her hand under its belly. It mewled again but came along as she lifted it, like so much defenseless meat.

"Sorry," she whispered, dropping it into the pillowcase. She couldn't have it touching Jacob or his medicine—who knew what germs it had—but she also couldn't bring herself to simply leave it there.

She went to the kitchen and stuffed a few snacks and the milk into the medicine bag, which was now full to bursting. Her phone was nowhere to be found, probably destroyed earlier by one of the men. After first surveying the large block table still barring the basement door, she looked wistfully to the front door, wishing it could be an option. It wasn't. An image of forcing that door open over Mark's chewed remains came to mind even as she leaned against the table, pushing slowly. It scraped against the floor, and she found herself going "shhh," as if it could heed her. The wolf pup yipped in the pillowcase.

Then the shower water turned off.

32

THE CHASE

Eleni was out of time.

She pushed the table aside, rough, not caring about the scraping sound it made. She heard a sharp "*hey!*" coming from the bathroom, yanked open the destroyed basement door (it quivered, barely holding itself together), and clopped rapidly down the wooden boards into the full darkness of the basement. The wolf pup swayed in the pillowcase. Jacob's fists clenched at her heavy coat as he woke and burrowed his face as deeply as he could into her shoulder. She held the hand axe up at the ready.

Her eyes quickly swept over the black of the basement, barely able to make out the shape of the generator and the outline of the cellar doors. She ran to them, hearing Ben's frantic, limping footfalls on the living room floor. Wedging her shoulder against a cellar door and using her shaking legs to push up with all her might, she forced one of the doors open and was hit full force with an icy gust of air as it swung out.

The effort it took cost her precious seconds.

A fast look around outside. Nothing moving that she could see. It was still dark out, but a silvery glow spread throughout the woods, hinting that sunlight was coming soon. The wolves were still circling up front near Mark's remains, the blood magnetic.

They'd smell the blood on her if the wind carried her scent in their direction.

She ran, over a mess of brambles a few feet from the door, toward the worn, narrow trail that she knew was back there. Ben had walked that trail with her in the sunlight as they held hands, headed for the fjord, the seaplane, and a picnic lunch they'd take out on the water. It was here, somewhere, that she took those steps with him, but the path was now covered with shadows and freshly fallen snow.

Her run took her through low shrubs and back into the cover of the trees. When two seconds later, she heard, "*Get back here!*" booming from the open cellar doors, she knew Ben wouldn't be able to get a clear shot at her. Not from there. She ran full-tilt, blood squishing in the boot of her injured foot. She no longer worried about being identified as prey. She'd already been identified. If it came to it, she'd simply have to show she was more than that.

She found the trail, or what she was reasonably sure was the trail. A wider gap between trees pointed in a nearly straight line toward the fjord. Certain she hadn't been turned around, she pushed herself to go even faster, the medicine bag and pillowcase banging into her sides. The wolf pup was making sounds, upset. Jacob, jostled by every step she took, was groaning.

She heard fast breath to her side, too close to be Ben. Her neck swiveled right and left, catching glimpses of dark, moving shapes. They recalled the ones she saw the night before, the sinister, running shadows that raced parallel to Chaz's car. Now, there was no steel and glass between them, no heater humming, keeping her and Jacob toasty. No small oasis of warmth in the night.

No, they were now fully out, tearing through the woods. She ran side by side with wild animals.

Ben continued to shout and yell behind her. A loud bang went off as he fired the gun, unsteady, and she heard a wolf's whimper. The gun fired again, and she was sure that this time, it was for her. She kept on. He was far enough behind, fighting for motion on his demolished leg, that she knew she could make it to the seaplane well ahead of him.

Then a large, black shape lunged onto the path directly in front of her, skidding on its planted paws. The fur on its back stuck up, its back arched and its entire being ready to strike and rip off her flesh. Eleni halted in her tracks, nearly spilling forward on top of Jacob and the hard, snow-covered, rocky ground. The wolf's eyes flashed in the dissipating night. She maintained eye contact and backed up a step or two, imagining another member of the pack tackling her from behind.

It didn't.

Instead, what felt like a sharp fire poker, fully heated, tore through her upper right bicep. The sleeve of her winter coat exploded with a puff of stuffing, and a burst of her blood erupted outward, painting the ragged opening. Her scream quickly followed the blast of the gun.

She fell forward after all, dropping the hand axe so she could instead stop herself and Jacob from slamming to the ground. Her right hand hit the surface defensively but gave way in less than an instant, the pain from her bicep going in a lightning ripple down to her wrist and making the entire arm collapse. Jacob went out of her grip, propelled forward and away from her into the snow, twisting in the air and whacking his forehead on a rock. The wolf pup scrambled out of the pillowcase, under Eleni's legs, and disappeared.

Another blast, and the large, adult wolf in front of her shrieked in pain and darted off into the woods. Jacob wailed.

Eleni floundered in the snow like a beached fish. She scrambled with her good hand, as if she were trying to climb a horizontal ladder over the ground toward her son. Her hand was on Jacob's foot when she heard the cock of the gun behind her, like ice cracking.

"Don't move," Ben instructed her.

33

THE CONFRONTATION

Eleni did as she was told, frozen in the snow. Her eyes were still on Jacob, though, who lay bawling at the end of her outstretched arm.

"Turn around."

She did as Ben said, purposely turning in the direction of her fallen hand axe to see where it had gone. Its handle stuck up from a mound of disturbed snow.

Her eyes trailed over the weapon and continued around in a smooth progress. Reclined on her good arm, she looked up at Ben.

She knew the look on his face must have been the same look he had when he killed Aimee.

He was still ten feet away, moving closer. His hair was dripping wet, frost quickly forming. The blood had been scrubbed from his face; the only hint that it had been there was a bit of missed red by his left ear. His breath exhaled in paper-white gusts. The splint and the knee splitter over his pants were only partially cleansed of blood. He'd yanked his thin, long-sleeved t-shirt back on—the same one he'd worn into the bathroom—but hadn't bothered to towel off or put on a coat. There hadn't been time. The shirt clung to him as a wet second skin.

He'd freeze to death if he stayed out here even thirty minutes, she was sure of it.

"Come here," he said. "Hands up."

She put her hands up, the hand on the arm that had been shot not reaching as high, then turned to look at Jacob.

"Ah-bup-bup!" Ben yelled. "Leave him!"

She looked back at Ben. The slight hesitation enraged him.

With a jerk, he took his gun's aim off of her and directed it at Jacob.

"Over here, right now, or he's dead!"

Jacob had blood trickling down into his eyes from the wound on his forehead. He swatted at his eyes furiously, the blood blocking his vision.

"He wasn't my idea anyway," Ben said.

Eleni was on her feet as quickly as she could be, hands up, following every instruction. Somewhere in the periphery of her vision, the wolf pup moved around in the snow.

"Get over here!"

She moved toward him, painfully conscious of how the hand axe was left behind.

Her feet dragged as she cast one more glance toward her baby, who was half-crawling after her, staying close.

"Hey! You choose him, he dies! You got it?"

Keeping her eyes on Ben, she moved toward him, but her ears were attuned to Jacob. To his breathing. She listened for the hitch, and when there was none, something in her was able to shift more fully, completely, to the task at hand.

The expectation was that she would pick Ben.

The expectation was always that she'd pick Ben. Even over herself.

Even, now, over her child, who she thought of as more than herself.

All those paltry, pitiful fantasies of being a "goddess" to Ben flashed through her mind. If she'd ever been a goddess to anybody, it had been to Jacob. She'd been a whole world to him. This little boy, all night long, had sought her out in the midst of so much horror and was soothed just at the sight of her. She loved him more fiercely than she'd even known.

Another step closer.

"Shame on you. Shame on you, Eleni," Ben said, spit spewing from his lips, which were contorted from his pain and his outrage.

She wanted to ask why Ben still wanted her but knew the answer.

He didn't really want her. He just wanted not to lose.

It was unthinkable to him that she'd be alive somewhere, no longer loving him, when she'd loved him once before. Unbearable for him to know she knew what he really was.

He hadn't wanted to know that Aimee knew what he was either.

These women served a purpose when they saw him the way he wanted to see himself: strong, smart, perfect. In charge. The boss.

When they didn't see him that way anymore, it was an assault on him. It was an attempt on his life. At least, the life he imagined he had. The person he imagined he was.

Eleni wasn't who she'd imagined either.

She was stronger than that person.

And as she closed the gap between her and Ben, every step making it more and more evident how much bigger he was than she, how much more crazed, she kept eye contact. Not simply to follow his orders and not to avoid triggering a predatory instinct in him . . .

To warn him that she herself was the threat.

She was the predator now. Teeth, claws, and millions of years of instinct surged through her. She was the mother wolf stalking her prey.

When less than three feet stood between them, Eleni lunged at him, springing off her strong legs. Her upraised hand caught his wrist, the one holding the gun, and it fired up into the sky as his arm went back.

Simultaneously, she raised her knee to her chest and kicked out and down. Real momentum surged behind the kick, and her angled heel hit him squarely in his already annihilated knee. The kick went between the slats of his splint, right in the front. He howled. The splint cracked and gave way. The knee inverted. She kicked at it over and over.

He fell back into the snow, on the rocks, and Eleni could see wolves just a little way off, her pack, waiting for the scraps she would throw them. Waiting for breakfast.

The silver tint to the light grew more pronounced, illuminating each tree, rock, animal, and spot of blood on the snow. Ben dropped his gun as he crashed down. Eleni dug her heel deep into his separating knee, twisted it, and spit at him.

"You're pathetic," she said. He thrashed on the ground, and she turned. She took up her axe, then her baby. If she wanted to, she could bring this axe down right into Ben's throat, but she didn't want to or need to. He was finished. It *was* pathetic. She didn't need to kill him; she only needed to walk away.

At a quick clip, she took off down the path, but her bearing had something of a regality to it. He roared her name as she left. She moved swiftly, still aware of the present danger, but not in a panic, not fleeing. He was nothing to her. It was over.

She knew it, even if he didn't, as he scrambled in the snow and once again found his gun.

34

THE RUN

Eleni was again observing the world from her hyper-alert state. The adrenaline from earlier in the night was back, crystallizing everything, making it clearer than clear. She saw every movement in the trees, heard the crack of every twig and the crunch of every dead leaf. It was amazing. Though she moved quickly through the woods with perfect animal precision, the wolves weren't after her. It was true—they went after weakness, and the weakness right now wasn't her own.

Behind her, and getting farther behind, lay Ben, still struggling to regain his footing. His yells, so authoritarian earlier, were devolving into increasingly high-pitched shrieks, and Eleni knew that the shrieks would soon be extinguished altogether.

His cries reached their crescendo when a wolf bit down hard into his already pulpy leg. He held that scream for a long time, and even though she didn't look back, she pictured his face snapping up to the sky, bright red, and the cords on his neck standing out so far that his neck seemed wider than his skull. She heard a wolf's snarl. Blood bubbled and popped as the beast breathed hard into it through its nose, wrestling back and forth with whatever bit of Ben's flesh it wanted to remove.

Ben took up his gun from the snow and fired. There was no yelp. The wolf was killed too quickly for it to even cry out.

Eleni kept going farther down the path. Jacob bounced in her arms, huffs of his tearful breath punctuating each step. Ben screamed her name, and it was a mix of fury and a plea for help. "*El-en-iiiii!*" In the woods, in the dim light, it didn't really sound like a name. It sounded like a dying animal's banshee howl, just a string of noises forced from the gut without logic.

She kept going and could see the seaplane now, docked at the end of the path. The old dock was partially gone, and what was left of it was rotting. Thick, ice-coated lichen infected every crevice of wood, but the fjord gleamed silver behind it. The body of the plane was much as she remembered, though the off-white paint with its red pipings was faded and chipped, partially painted over in a camouflage green. She noticed the area on the back, right below the tail, had been scraped completely clean of its paint, leaving only a wide swath of dull chrome. That was where the plane's serial number had been.

Noises sounded behind her, and even though they were at least fifty feet back, she knew they weren't the noises of wolves. The wolves were light, built with exacting paws that touched down and bounded up, bodies that weaved like mist in and out of the space within the brush. These sounds were heavy, uncoordinated, pained. Limbs dragged clumps of snow along with them as they were pulled over the ground. Hands gripped at rocks and branches, pulling. There was nothing elegant or canine in these sounds.

Eleni stepped onto the decaying planks of the dock. Then she saw:

The boat was chained to an old, rusted metal loop that had been bolted to one corner above a clump of foamy green plants glazed with sparkling frost.

Hoisting Jacob again and balancing him on her forearm, she transferred the hand axe to the hand beneath him, unzipped her jacket, and dug the keys to the seaplane out of her sweatshirt pocket. Two keys. She bent to the worn padlock and tried one, then the other, already knowing they wouldn't work. One was the key to the cabin, the other, the key to the plane. The key to the lock on the chain wasn't there.

"Mommy," Jacob whispered in her ear, "Daddy's coming."

She looked back, and forty feet away was Ben, half-crouching on his good leg, somewhat bear-crawling with that leg and his two arms. The bad leg was dragging behind, bumping over the uneven terrain, useless. The dead meat was still attached to its host.

He smiled at her, giving a half-chuckle, half-scream. His blood was smeared over his front teeth.

She knew the key to that chain was somewhere on him. Or perhaps even inside his coat, back in the cabin, still laying where Willie had thrown it after stripping it off Ben's frame.

It didn't matter.

"You can't get away!" Ben shrieked, then laughed.

She shoved the key into the lock on the seaplane door, and it took three tries—

But then the key turned, the old lock clicking against its internal rust, and the door opened with the sound of banging metal.

A small shape, one that had been trotting along as best it could on its uncertain legs, out of Ben's reach, stepped onto the dock. Eleni's brain took in that information. She put Jacob into the plane, on the padded seat with stuffing leaking from the seams. Her injured bicep ached and failed her, but she still managed with her other arm. She bent to scoop the wolf pup who had followed her amidst the chaos and put it in on the plane floor.

Ben hobbled quickly now, spurred on by the madness boiling in his brain and the sight of Eleni growing nearer . . . the sight of Eleni restricted by a chain. Eleni, without a gun, had only a small axe and was not close enough to use it.

"I win! You're pathetic! *You're* pathetic!" he screeched, shrill, latching on to her own word to throw back at her in an attempt to cancel out what she'd said.

Eleni climbed into the plane, pulling herself with her good arm, the other one going numb as it hung by her side. Jacob, still sniffling, crawled across the flat seat to the passenger side. The wolf pup circled around Eleni's ankles as she got herself seated upright.

Ben was only ten feet away when she reached out, grabbed the thick plastic strap bolted to the door, and pulled it shut with all her might. It closed with a heavy thud, like a car trunk, then Ben banged on the window with the butt of his gun, fumbling at the handle.

"You're not going anywhere! You're not going anywhere!" he yelled, the yell becoming a chant. Eleni looked hopelessly over the endless array of buttons and levers. He taught her this—they'd done this together three and a half years ago. But her mind went blank.

Then she had it. Maneuvering to use her good arm, she grabbed a hold of the large black ball on the end of one of the central levers and began to pump the lever up and down. A few moments later, there was a guttural, rusty groan from the engine, and the front propeller began to spin. The slow rotation built quickly, and soon, the choppy sight of the individual blades going by became a solid blurred circle.

"You're chained, idiot!" Ben yelled. He banged the window again, and a small crack appeared in the glass. Heartened, he hit it once more, and Eleni felt a few tiny shards pepper the side of her face as he made impact. The small crack spread into a wide, sinister-looking spiderweb of fractured glass.

Eleni worked the buttons and levers. The plane began to drift away from the dock. She heard a blast and a loud, metallic clang and realized Ben was shooting at the door handle.

The plane halted only a few feet out, the chain pulling taut.

Eleni reached over and forced Jacob back into a seated position. She pulled a seatbelt over him and fastened it, despite the fact he was too small for it.

Too late for that car seat now.

She pulled her own seat belt on.

"You're a monster," Ben shouted. "You're the worst person that ever lived. I'd be better off dead than with someone like you."

Eleni looked at him through the window. As soon as he caught her eye, he raised his gun, squinting for a perfect kill shot through the glass.

Dead's what you're gonna be, Ben.

She gave it everything she had. Full throttle. The chain against the metal leg of the plane groaned and scraped like claws ripping over a chalkboard as she made the plane spin wildly toward Ben. His shot went askew as he dropped to the dock, narrowly escaping the propeller. The metal loop gave, pulling from the rotting boards; the seaplane turned again to face out into the waterway. Ben stayed down on the planks to avoid the tail of the aircraft.

The plane puttered out into the fjord, gaining speed. Soon, it began to rise and fall. It rose up ten feet, then twenty, right as the sun broke over the mountains enveloping the water.

Eleni only looked back once. Ben was sitting, crippled, on the now-splintered dock, screaming up at her. She couldn't hear him.

But she could see three sleek, dark, canine shapes stalking him from behind.

35

THE PAYOFF

The sun was up, now at its highest point of the day. The fjord was brilliant, the sky as clear as Eleni ever remembered seeing it. Mountains capped in ice and snow shone like diamonds and sapphires, their ruts a deep blue. The trees that fully hemmed in the shores looked like meticulously trimmed Christmas trees with snow theatrically balanced on their branches.

Eleni had only briefly managed to get the seaplane airborne before it fell the short distance from the air and skimmed the water's surface, creating an impressive wake that rocked them for quite a while. It now bopped along tranquilly in the center of the fjord. The plane's noisy heater ran steadily, and Eleni didn't try to get up in the air again; risking a crash would be pointless. She knew that out here in the open, with Logan inevitably going by the cabin again and seeing the carnage, it was only a matter of time before she was found.

Jacob slept peacefully at her side, the seatbelt still slung around him. Soon after they'd fallen, semi-roughly, back into the water, Eleni had killed the propeller and dug some of her first aid materials out of the medicine bag. She'd lovingly wiped off his face as he sniffed, indignant at all he'd gone through. Relief coursed through her as strongly as adrenaline when she saw his injury was a minor scrape across the forehead that had bled far more excessively than was indicative of its severity.

"You've been through so much," she told him. "You were so brave. I'm so, so proud of you."

"Mommy so powed," Jacob said, dazed but pleased with her admiration. She hugged and kissed him for over an hour before he started to bat her away, wanting sleep again. However much of all this he'd remember, she knew it would be far more than she would have wished on him.

"May this be the worst thing you ever go through," she whispered to him once he was asleep. "May everything from here on be easier. May you be so strong, so brave, for what you've had to face and never have to face anything like it again."

It was a solid, steady mother's prayer, and she went on in that fashion for quite a while. So long, in fact, that it became almost meditative, a spilling out that became like an incantation over her son's prone body. Prone but finally safe.

As they drifted, she marveled at the beauty all around them. She searched the shore to see if she could spot Ben's dock, so tiny and purposely obscured. She couldn't. Gazing at the thick blanket of trees all along the coast, she thought of how just last night, less than twenty-four hours ago, they'd been in Chaz's car. They'd picked their way through the woods with no visibility, moving forward with zero certainty. Now, all around her was like smooth glass, utterly clear and freeing. She felt she could cross the world.

Far ahead, she saw something breach the surface. Whales, common all throughout the area.

Her bullet wound was superficial. She'd washed it out as best she could in the seaplane, briefly opening the door and stepping down to balance on one of the large floats that supported them to scoop some frigid water into her hand. The glacier water was pristine. She'd sloshed it into her wound, then stuffed the gash with cotton tufts pulled from her torn coat before unclipping the detachable strap from the medicine bag to tie it tight over the gash.

She thought of Ben's mother then, for some reason, and the thought surprised her since she'd rarely ever thought of the woman before. She was alive somewhere down in Oregon. Ben and she had been estranged, and while Eleni had made a half-hearted attempt to contact her in the wake of Ben's disappearance, the woman never reached out.

What had their life been like together? Ben's father hadn't died until Ben was about fifteen. Had the two of them been abused? Had Ben decided to hate his own mother because she made attempts at disciplining him? Eleni had no idea.

At her ankles, the wolf pup stood, circled, and lay down again, happy to drift in and out of sleep as they floated peacefully on the water. Once things had calmed down and Jacob's face was clean, an Elmo BAND-AID secured over his cut, Eleni had thought of the animal. The pup was bounced around during their brief flight but seemed to simply curl into a fuzzy ball and come out of it all right. Eleni, with no dish or anything to use, poured some of the milk she'd brought into her own cupped hand and allowed the pup to lick it out. She knew little about wolves but wondered if her own scent wasn't fast becoming associated with "mother," in the absence of its own mother. After, she poured a generous amount of hand sanitizer over her palm, and it dripped to the floor as she rubbed her hands together. The pup wasn't allowed up on the seat with them.

She thought of the pup's mom, now cold on the floor of the cabin, the fire long-since died out. Imagining the chilled grey light in the cabin as it fought to filter through the trees and windows was easy. The cellar doors and basement door would have been left wide open. She wondered if other animals found their way inside, perhaps wolves in mourning, sniffing and prodding at the blue, blood-soaked sheet with their noses. Maybe they'd start to gnaw on Arlen and Willie.

Exactly how much would be left of any of them by the time Logan found them?

Perhaps he'd found them already, put their remains into metal boxes, and carried them out of that place.

"I'm going to do all I can to make sure you're the best person you can be," Eleni said over Jacob, a new line in her string of mom-prayers. She had no idea what Ben's childhood was like or if men like this were born of nature or nurture or both. But she would do everything, absolutely everything she could, to see that Jacob became a good man.

The wolf pup snarled and tugged at something under the seat—an ancient duffel bag, its woven handle frayed in multiple places. The pup added to the fraying through the work of its tiny teeth. Eleni leaned forward, her spoken Jacob-wish mantras halting here and there as she bent and squished her diaphragm. She pulled the duffel bag out and looked it over, curious, then unzipped it.

Stacks of cash bound together with paper bracelets, the kind you'd get for admission to a theme park, jostled over and around each other as the zipper unzipped. Eleni saw the number "100" repeated over and over again from different angles. Her mantras slowed and then stopped completely. She'd lost her breath and couldn't speak. Re-zipping the bag, she sat back and looked out the window for a long time.

Eventually, she pulled the wolf mother's tooth out of her sweatshirt pocket, turning it over and over between her fingers.

Jacob stirred in his sleep, and she gave him her other hand. He grabbed her index finger and pulled it close to him, as if he'd grabbed the corner of a beloved security blanket.

Somewhere, obscured by the mountains, another seaplane started its propeller. She could hear the almost imperceptible whirring of the blades as they gained momentum. Despite the obstacles between them, she knew it was coming. She knew she was found.

EPILOGUE

Eleni carefully navigated the gangplank from the ferry to the wooden dock. Her strappy sandals weren't sensible, but they were the ones she'd envisioned wearing. Her foot—the one that had gone through the teeth of the knee splitter and lived to show it—had some noticeable scars, like thick, white tracings. The scars were visible in her sandals, but she didn't care. Her dress, white with some coral-colored flowers, blew about her legs in the wind. It was perhaps still too cold—even in June—for a sundress, despite the heavy, coral cardigan she pulled tightly around her torso.

She'd made a point of dressing up almost every day for the past month. Staring at the mounds of sweats in her recovered luggage, she felt claustrophobic at the thought of putting them on, like she'd be burying herself. The stores in Juneau were now accustomed to seeing her out, routinely looking for new clothes.

Jacob held her hand, staring in fascination at the rippling water beneath the gangplank. He wore a light blue, collared shirt that was dotted with tiny white whales under a pair of overalls.

With Eleni's other hand, she held a thick, leather leash. Sasha, their wolf pup, getting bigger every day, trotted alongside them.

Officer Pete Logan, true to his word, waited for them on the dock.

"Hey, there he is!" Pete cheered, looking at Jacob, who beamed under the attention, even as he half-cowered behind his mother's leg. Eleni laughed, savoring the feel of the breeze blowing her hair back over her shoulders. Her hand went to her throat and to the tooth of the wolf mother, which now hung there on a chain, having been fixed with a gold loop by a jeweler in Juneau. She wore it constantly, rubbing her thumb in its curved groove as if it were a worry stone.

"Here he is. Superstar boy," she said.

She'd stayed in town for over a month after Pete found her and Jacob bobbing in the seaplane. Pete set them up in a vacant apartment owned by a friend of his; it was not quite the witness protection program, but it would do as all the dust settled and inquiries took place around what had happened in the cabin. She'd reported Chaz, who was soon after arrested as an accomplice to Arlen, Willie, and Mark—though not before he figured out where Eleni was staying and stopped by to threaten and berate her.

"You were already there," he'd sputtered, an attempt at an apology before her silence caused him to dissolve into screamed insults. "You were there, and they showed up. What else was I gonna do?"

Not take the money. Call the cops after they left. Not shrug off what you knew could be three murders, one of an innocent child.

She had the sense to record it all on her phone, which would not help his case.

He was now awaiting trial. Eleni would have to testify. It was one of the reasons she was back to meet with Pete. That—and to discuss a few technical things.

She turned the money she found in the seaplane over to the police. All of it. She knew it was blood money and wanted no part of it. She hadn't expected to receive a reward from both the states of Alaska and Oregon. She also hadn't expected, upon Ben's presumed "death," to inherit all that she did.

Ben put everything in her name when he disappeared. She'd always known that and knew he did it as a safety precaution. Out of everyone in the world, he knew she wouldn't touch one red cent. And she hadn't. But now that he was no longer considered "missing," everything had fully transferred over to her. There were things she hadn't even known existed: properties in various states. Likely places he'd acquired while trafficking drugs, Pete said, although Ben had been smart enough to make it difficult to trace the funds with which he'd purchased the homes to illegal activity. The deeds had been tucked away in the chimney, along with the photo of and letters from Aimee, all of which the police found when Eleni told them where to look. There was also the cabin and the seaplane and an overseas bank account with over six figures in it. He always told her he had nothing. When they fantasized together about their lives, he'd always stressed how he couldn't contribute much financially. The reality that he had more money than Eleni ever fathomed boggled her mind.

She knew exactly what she wanted to do with it.

The building she'd found in Juneau was a motel-turned-apartment-complex with eighteen units (nine upstairs, nine down) and an office with its own adjoining apartment. It stood empty for a number of years, with most of the windows smashed and plywood boards nailed up in their place. The back of the building was scrawled with graffiti, but that could be removed, and each unit had its own kitchenette and full bathroom. An old hotel in town, preparing to do full renovations, was willing to donate eighteen lightly used bedroom sets for her cause.

It was perfect.

"Got something for you," Pete said, looking down at Jacob. From behind his back, he pulled a hybrid dinosaur-truck toy. Jacob squealed with delight, holding out his hand. Pete gave it over.

She had trouble explaining exactly why she'd chosen to stay in Alaska. She didn't want to live too near to where the cabin was, yet she couldn't see herself going back to the little studio apartment in Washington. It felt too closely connected with the old her. The ghost of the imaginary Ben, who she'd so often pictured there, admiring her solo parenting, was too prevalent. Choices that compromised her were too palpable. She'd wound up giving her notice at work, selling her things, and finding a place in Juneau.

Pete walked them to the tiny police station. Kent, the officer who had questioned her long ago, briefly passed them on their way in and gave the same nod-as-if-to-tip-his-hat to Eleni that Pete once had.

As Eleni lowered herself into the metal chair with the cushioned seat, she experienced a strong wave of déjà vu. Jacob now sat in the same chair that Ben sat in when they'd come to give her statement, and apart from the new calendar right over Pete's shoulder, everything else had stayed the same. She went over a few documents pertaining to the upcoming trial. In a plastic evidence bag, she got the keys to the cabin back.

"Do you want to go see it?" Pete asked her, his eyes downcast as if he was embarrassed to ask.

Eleni thought for a moment.

"That's not what today's about."

She smiled at Jacob. He held up his new toy, which he'd been playing with throughout the entire meeting.

"Its wheels roar, Mommy," he exclaimed proudly, as if Eleni hadn't heard them roar repeatedly as she and Pete worked.

"So cool," she said.

She knew she'd be back to the cabin to clean it out and look it over. Her intent was to sell it, along with the seaplane, if there was anyone who'd want it. She was fairly sure, given the adventurous spirit of this place, a buyer would come along. But she wasn't ready yet; maybe, by the end of the summer, she would be.

Curled up around her feet, Sasha licked Eleni's ankles. It wasn't too unusual for someone in Alaska to have a domesticated wolf as a pet. It wasn't exactly common, but it certainly wasn't unheard of. Eleni considered sending Sasha to live in a special wildlife preserve and never trusted the wolf any farther than she could see her. Sasha perpetually stayed outside and Jacob never played with her. The wolf and the child were also never alone together. The animal obeyed Eleni completely, and sometimes Eleni would sit and just marvel at how, with each passing day, Sasha looked more and more like the wolf mother that had been shot and killed in the cabin.

Toward the very end of their meeting, Pete took out a small metal box. It was three inches wide on each side, two inches deep. It had a small, brass lock on the front, its only adornment. A key sat in the lock.

"So, there he is," Pete said, solemn. Eleni had known it was coming.

They never found Ben's remains. At least, not all of them. They found the lower left leg, fully separated from the pulverized knee, stuck to the ground in a pool of frozen blood a few feet from the trail. Most of the meat had been chewed off, the tibia chipped with teeth marks.

"Anything could've happened," Pete had told her over coffee in her small apartment about a week or two after that night. "They ate him up and buried the other bones. They dragged him down into a den somewhere. Hell, he might've just fallen in the fjord. There's stuff in there that'll eat you up, too, for sure."

It wasn't a full body, but it was enough for the police to pronounce Ben dead. Their knowledge of the elements in Alaska in March, the fact he was last seen being attacked by wolves, and the fact that, if nothing else, he had lost a leg and been bleeding out, made them certain he hadn't survived. Now, Eleni was just going through the painstaking legalities of wrapping up all the technical ends of his life.

She was, in a way, like his widow.

In the small tin box were the ashes from that found leg, given to her as "next of kin."

"There he is," she said, reaching out and sliding the locked box fully to her edge of the desk. Then she let go of it and kept her hands folded in her lap. She stared at the box but didn't really want to touch it.

After the initial police search of the cabin, she had been shown the letter Willie had written—the one Arlen had intended to nail to her chest for Ben to find. It simply read, "This is because of you. If you don't want the same thing to happen to the kid, come and find us."

Because of you.

Once or twice, Pete had asked her about Ben, not in an official police way, but conversationally, talking in the apartment. She'd felt herself withdraw. Broaching the subject was like reaching out to touch tender, bruised flesh—her fingers could barely press upon it before she had to pull away.

Pete never pressed too hard.

"So," Pete now said, awkwardness filling the air, "I'd love to take you both to lunch if you'd like? Get Jacob some ice cream?"

Eleni smiled, and it was a genuine smile. She liked Pete. In fact, for the first time since that summer with Ben, she could see herself becoming romantically involved with someone. There had been a night in the apartment he'd set her up in when he'd come to brief her on updates in the case. Leaning over endless papers, it had suddenly seemed like he was about to kiss her. He'd wanted to, she was fairly certain. But he'd stopped himself. It would have been unprofessional, and she'd come to learn he was meticulously professional.

This budding relationship was so different from the one she'd experienced before. There was no desperate need to please, no pressure or dramatic mood swings masquerading

EPILOGUE

as passion. There was only an interest, an enjoyment. They shared an easy attraction that helped build her up.

There was, also, some fear. She feared making the same mistake twice. It was a fear that she recognized inside herself and one she would work through.

"I'd love to. I really would," she said and meant it. "But . . ." she looked at Jacob, expectant.

"Train ride!" Jacob said.

She laughed. "For his birthday, I'm taking him on the train. He's developing a thing for trains."

"No kidding, up on the White Pass? You're a lucky guy, buddy."

"Some special Mommy-Jacob time," she said affectionately. She tousled Jacob's hair. Only the faintest white scratch on his forehead, usually covered by his bangs, remained of the gash he got in the woods. Nightmares had plagued him since that terrible night. He fell asleep curled close to Eleni and panicked if she left the room without him, even just to use the restroom. It was getting better, though. Eleni took him to see counselors, people who specialized in this type of trauma and in children this small.

"He's honestly coping so, so well," they told her. "You've done a great job talking about it with him, helping him have a frame of reference that's appropriate for his age."

Jacob shook his dino-truck excitedly, making it roar.

"He has an amazing mother," Pete said, looking at her now.

She felt herself blush. In the past, she might have said no or shrugged . . . something to indicate she wasn't all that great. Now, though, she simply said, "Thank you."

Eleni had also spoken to counselors since that night three months ago. She'd also had nightmares and moments of panic. In addition to coping with the trauma, she worried about coming under fire from the law too. After all, she had gone to meet Ben without informing authorities.

"Given the circumstances, the chances of you being charged with anything are remote," Pete had reassured her. Still, the concern would resurface at odd moments.

All this, but, deep down, something in her felt more settled and good than it had in her entire life.

Before Pete walked them out, she told him they'd be staying in town that night and catching the ferry back to Juneau the next afternoon. They made plans to have lunch before they left.

The day after that, she'd go look at the building she'd found in Juneau. The one she planned to turn into a safe house for people fleeing abusive relationships, people who had nowhere to go. She could think of no more fitting outlet for the money that had come to her.

"I'll want to come back before the summer's over," she told Pete. "To clean out the cabin. Put it on the market."

"I'll be happy to take you out—when you're ready."

She nodded. The small tin box was clasped in her hands now as they stood right outside the police station. Small tundra planes took off behind them on the single runway of the town's tiny, security-less airport. The depot for the train was only a few blocks away.

Pete took Sasha's leash, having agreed to keep her at the station until they got back from their ride. He often held on to Sasha for them when they needed to go somewhere.

"What will you do with him?" Pete asked, nodding at the box.

"Do people hold funerals for legs?"

Pete chuckled in spite of himself. "Guess you can hold a funeral for anything you want to say bye to."

She nodded.

Later that afternoon, the tour guide on the train led the tourists in a round of "Happy Birthday" for Jacob and brought out a special piece of cake. Eleni had organized it earlier. Some of the people working on the train still remembered her, although turnover of tour guides was almost yearly. Even the manager who once cautioned her against Ben had already left for another job.

When the train reached the pinnacle of its journey and stood idling beside a crystal-clear mountaintop lake so passengers could take all the pictures their hearts desired, Eleni carried Jacob out onto the back platform to breathe in the fresh air.

"So, wait," she teased him. "How old are you now? *How* old?"

"Three!" he squealed, gleeful at the game.

"No way. It can't be."

"Way, Mommy!"

"You're such a big boy!" she said and gave him a huge kiss on the cheek. "A big boy and a good boy."

All along the train tracks, the whole way up, it was possible to spot debris from the Klondike Gold Rush. Old tools used to build the railroad, then abandoned, remained untouched amid the rocks. They were things made of steel and iron that had stood the test of time in the brutal elements.

She stared at a rut beside the lake, dotted with a few old bolts and a fully rusted railroad spike, then slipped the dull tin box from her pocket.

She could keep it with her. When she returned to the cabin in a month or two, she could scatter the ashes there. But something in her didn't want to bring them along when she went back down the mountain.

She put the box on the rail and turned the small brass key. Once it was open, she stared briefly at the clumped, gray ashes, then shook them out. The hand holding the box had a pinky finger checker-boarded with keloid scars.

The wind carried the ashes over the crystal lake.

"Dirty," Jacob said, making a silly face. Eleni laughed.

She looked at the box, looked around—then knocked it off the ledge. It landed off to the side and looked like any other long-lost, metal artifact along the tracks. Part of ancient history.

Which is exactly what it was.
She kissed Jacob's cheek.
Such a big boy. Such a good boy.
And I know that's because of me.

BOOK GROUP DISCUSSION GUIDE

1. The title *Wolves at Night* has several meanings. What is your interpretation of the title?

2. When Eleni looks back at her "summer of romance" with Ben, there are several warning signs that this is not a healthy relationship. What warning signs did you notice?

3. In another flashback, Eleni recalls having to give a statement to the police after Ben got into a physical altercation with another man. The cop taking the statement mostly listens to Ben and takes Eleni's silence as agreement with what Ben says, rather than encouraging her to speak on her own. What is the significance of this? Have you had similar experiences?

4. There are two police officers mentioned in the story—Kent and Logan. How do they each approach Eleni differently?

5. How might Ben's character and his relationship with Eleni be mirrored in the metaphor of the cabin?

6. At times, Eleni seems to willfully ignore red flags in her relationship with Ben. Why? And why do people in real-life abusive situations sometimes do this?

7. In Chapter 18, Eleni realizes that "the confusion of it, the not knowing the right thing to say, the how to get out, was the worst part." In Chapter 29, she thinks about other relationships Ben may have had where he left the women "blaming themselves for wrongs they never actually committed." How do these lines reflect emotionally abusive situations? What is emotional abuse?

8. At some point, Eleni begins to work instinctually vs intellectually. Where does this point occur, and why?

9. *Wolves at Night* contains many parallels between people and animals. Which ones did you notice? When is the link of humans to animals empowering, and when is it frightening?

10. In Chapter 23, Eleni realizes "they can only torment you if they're in control." Discuss the importance of control in abusive relationships. In what ways does Eleni take control back?

11. Eleni has a memory of a grade-school friend who said her name, which sounds like "L.N.E.," could stand for "lost, not erased." What is the significance of this memory?

12. Does Eleni actually love Ben? Does Ben actually love Eleni?

13. Eleni's own childhood and family life are barely acknowledged. The most significant mention of it comes toward the end of the novel when it's revealed in just one sentence that Eleni's father hit her mother. What is the significance of this? Does the fact that Eleni refused to think about her parents for the majority of the story tell you anything about how she copes with things?

14. Is Eleni a good mother at the start of the story? At the end? Why or why not?

15. Eleni's parents do not really recognize Jacob as their grandson and rejected her for becoming pregnant while unmarried. How does this factor into Eleni's decision to go to the cabin?

16. The most important part of love, to Ben, is that it be "unwavering." What does unwavering mean to him? How does his view of love differ from Eleni's?

17. Does Ben really want to be with Eleni? If not, what are his true psychological motivations for needing to hold on to her?

18. In Chapter 31, Eleni thinks about how she was tricked into wanting to preserve her submissiveness as if it were a virtue. What does this mean? How was she "tricked?" Is this an abusive technique?

19. What are the key ways in which Eleni changes throughout the story?

20. Do you believe Eleni will have another romantic relationship in the future? If so, how will she approach it?

21. How does being a mother make Eleni simultaneously stronger and more vulnerable?

22. Are women, in general, more likely to be taken advantage of simply because they bear children? Why or why not?

23. Eleni recalls a time when Jacob remarked, casually, that he doesn't have a father. While this made her feel guilty, did Jacob seem to mind that there was no father in his life?

24. Had Ben been there at Jacob's birth and raised him with Eleni, how do you think Jacob's life and upbringing would have been different? How might Eleni have developed differently as a mother?

25. This story is riddled with characters who behave badly in a variety of ways. Arlen is an obvious villain, but people like Janine also do things that are wrong. Discuss how other characters' misdeeds enable Eleni to excuse Ben's actions or to stay with him.

26. Arlen accuses Ben of being a worse villain because Ben pretends to be good. Do you agree that this makes Ben worse?

27. Eleni has a talent for making things seem fine when they aren't. Can you relate to this? How is this talent a negative?

28. How do you think the mindsets behind emotional abuse and physical abuse are the same? Are different types of abuse triggered in the same ways?

29. Logan calls Eleni brave for being a single mother. It's such a contrast to the things other people in her life have said about her that it gives her a moment's pause. Have you ever had something in your life that people viewed negatively, when in actuality, it showed a positive attribute?

30. Chapter 23 is titled "The Broken Knee (and the Broken Back)." What does this title mean?

31. Do you believe Ben assaulted Janine? Did you believe it when Janine first said it, before finishing the novel? Why or why not?

32. Aimee Hart is an enigmatic figure. What do you think her home life was like? Her relationship with Ben? What struck you most about her story?

33. Which scene or passage stuck with you the most? Why?

34. What was your favorite part? Least favorite? Which part was most upsetting or emotional for you?

ABOUT THE AUTHOR

Sara McDermott Jain is an award-winning, produced screenwriter and published author. Her passion is moving readers through fear and into empowerment via the thriller and horror genres. She is also the creator of the Book to Script Course, which shows authors how to adapt their books into screenplays (www.booktoscriptcourse.com), and she teaches both screenwriting and novel writing at the college level. To learn more about Sara, visit www.saramcdermottjain.com.

THANK YOU!

There are many amazing people in my life who deserve thanks. We're impacted by everything around us, in ways both good and bad, and below is a list of those people who have had a wonderful impact on me. In no particular order, I thank each and every one of them with all my heart for helping me to achieve this milestone!

1. To Kary Oberbrunner, who has inspired me not just through AAE but through his friendship. You're changing the lives of so many people by helping them tell their stories!

2. To my editors, Tina Morlock and Diana L. James, whose brilliant insight and support helped to refine this book and share its message.

3. To Corrie Johnson for shepherding me through the publication process.

4. To Debbie O'Byrne, cover designer extraordinaire, for her beautiful work on this book.

5. To my 7th grade English teacher, Mary Reindorp, who first said she thought I was a writer and could be published.

6. To Emily Farrell, my high school creative writing teacher. I took your course every year and would have taken it forever if I could! Thank you for all you taught me.

7. To Donna Zytko, who helped me through so much of the wilderness in my own life.

8. To my parents, George and Judy McDermott, who, when an elementary school teacher told them she was afraid I was the "artsy type," completely embraced it and let me be me. To this day, they still aid me in achieving my dreams.

9. To my sister, Missy, who is always my first reader.

10. To my brother, Matt, a constant source of love and support.

11. To Brendan Fanning, who believed in this book and helped keep me going until it was officially published.

12. To all my friends and colleagues who are so nurturing and supportive of what I want to do in my life.

13. To my son, Nicholas, the inspiration in all I do and the light in my world. I'd fight any number of wolves for you!

You've read the story;
now get your own **FREE**
Wolves Workbook . . .

The wolf symbolizes
power—when it's been
taken away from you and
when you've taken it back.
Use your free
Wolves Workbook
to explore the power
patterns in your life and
step into a stronger,
more powerful you!

Sign up at
www.saramcdermottjain.com/wolves
and get your free copy today.

If you or someone you know is suffering as a result of domestic violence, please contact the National Domestic Violence Hotline. Visit www.thehotline.org or call 1-800-799-SAFE for more information.